MW00648196
sank his teeth into
her bleeding neck.
"Aah!"
Then he sucked,
loud and hard.

Arnold touched his forehead to hers. There was a rustling sound as his hair brushed against hers. He closed his eyes.
"Please, don't cry anymore. I can't handle seeing you cry."
"Ngh..."

Rishe blanched as she
was lifted into the air.
Your Highness,
noooo!
"You just don't want to be
carried sideways, right?"

7th TIME LOOP

The Villainess Enjoys a Carefree Life Married to Her Worst Enemy!

NOVEL

3

WRITTEN BY

Touko Amekawa

ILLUSTRATED BY

Wan☆Hachipisu

Seven Seas Entertainment

7TH TIME LOOP: THE VILLAINESS ENJOYS A CAREFREE LIFE MARRIED TO HER WORST ENEMY! VOL. 3

Rūpu 7-kai-me no Akuyaku Reijō wa, Moto Tekikoku de Jiyū Kimamana Hanayome Seikatsu o Mankitsu suru Vol. 3

First published in Japan in 2021 by OVERLAP Inc., Ltd., Tokyo.
English translation rights arranged with OVERLAP Inc., Ltd., Tokyo.

Seven Seas press and purchase enquiries can be sent to Marketing Manager Lianne Sentar at press@gomanga.com. Information regarding the distribution and purchase of digital editions is available from Digital Manager CK Russell at digital@gomanga.com.

Follow Seven Seas Entertainment online at sevenseasentertainment.com.

TRANSLATION: Amy Osteraas
ADAPTATION: Vida Cruz-Borja
COVER DESIGN: H. Qi
INTERIOR LAYOUT & DESIGN: Clay Gardner
COPY EDITOR: Meg van Huygen
PROOFREADER: Jade Gardner
LIGHT NOVEL EDITOR: T. Anne
PREPRESS TECHNICIAN: Melanie Ujimori, Jules Valera
PRODUCTION MANAGER: Lissa Pattillo
EDITOR-IN-CHIEF: Julie Davis
ASSOCIATE PUBLISHER: Adam Arnold
PUBLISHER: Jason DeAngelis

ISBN: 978-1-63858-858-0
Printed in Canada
First Printing: April 2023
10 9 8 7 6 5 4 3 2 1

7TH TIME LOOP:
THE VILLAINESS ENJOYS A CAREFREE LIFE
MARRIED TO HER WORST ENEMY!

CHAPTER 1
9

CHAPTER 2
43

CHAPTER 3
91

CHAPTER 4
121

CHAPTER 5
145

CHAPTER 6
173

BONUS STORY
Without the Need for a Lullaby
235

CHAPTER 1

WHILE RISHE WALKED with Arnold to the party hall on the night he gave her the ring, a question rose in her mind.

"Why did you propose to me when you did, Prince Arnold?"

It was a question she'd asked him several times since they first met. He always dodged it, but she figured it was about time for the truth. She peered up at him expectantly but found that he was giving her a rather stern look in return.

Ever composed, he replied, "I believe I told you before. It was because I fell for you."

Come on, we both know that's a lie!

No matter how many times she reexamined their first meeting, she couldn't pinpoint what she'd done to endear her to Arnold. She certainly couldn't imagine Arnold Hein of all people proposing to a stranger on a mere whim.

Somewhat sulkily, Rishe mentioned the evidence she'd been holding on to for this conversation. "You also said you brought me here to use me."

"Well, the reason doesn't really matter, does it?"

Maybe not to you!

This was a big turning point in Rishe's life. She didn't need to know everything, but having a little more information would definitely help.

She made her dissatisfaction plain on her face, and Arnold laughed, evidently finding it amusing. At this rate, he'd never tell her the reason he proposed no matter what she did. Staring down at the band on her ring finger, Rishe made up her mind.

I think it's time to move on to the next stage in my plan.

***

"So, Prince Theodore, I'd really appreciate it if you could tell me about Prince Arnold's relationship with your father."

"You really cut to the chase sometimes, don't you?"

Theodore shot Rishe an exasperated look from where he was reclining on the grass. The sunlight must have been too bright for him because he rubbed his eyes after glancing up at her. He didn't seem very enthusiastic about answering her question, but still, he sat up and engaged with her. This made him just as kind as his brother in Rishe's book.

"As his fiancée, I should learn about him *and* his father." Rishe laid her handkerchief flat next to Theodore and sat on it, legs pressed together. "You know more about Prince Arnold than anyone else, which is why I've come to you in my time of need."

"Hee hee. Well, you're right about that. I'm the world's best resource for information on him."

Rishe applauded Theodore, who puffed up with pride. He put his elbow on his knee and rested his chin in his hand before continuing.

"Sorry to get your hopes up, but I don't think I can answer that question. Even if it's you who's asking, *and* even if you give me a new scoop on Arnold in return!"

"Why not?"

"I've never talked with my father. I've looked into what I could regarding him and my brother, but they don't speak in public, you see." Theodore plucked strands of grass as he spoke. "Even when our father has orders for him, Arnold is called to the audience chamber alone. Not even Oliver or our father's attendants are allowed at their meetings."

They only ever meet alone?

"I know a little about his mother, though."

Rishe snapped her head up at those unexpected words. "If I recall correctly, you and Prince Arnold have different mothers. Is that right?"

"It's not that uncommon, really."

She'd also heard that Theodore's mother had already passed. Galkhein's current empress was not a blood relation to either brother.

"Remember when I said Arnold killed his mother?" Theodore asked, face softening a little with sadness.

Rishe nodded and asked what she hadn't then: "What happened?"

"Arnold's mother always hated him. She kept him as far away

from her as possible. Whenever she saw him, she'd shower abuse on him. It went on like that for years until he finally stabbed her with a sword." Quietly, Theodore added, "Right through the heart."

That instant, Rishe remembered dying by Arnold's sword in her sixth life. Back then, he'd thrust his blade straight into *her* heart. "Do you know for sure that's what happened?"

"It was kept hidden from the public, but everybody who's anybody in this country knows about it." Theodore grimaced like he'd tasted something bitter. "His mother was royalty—and a hostage. Our father commanded her to marry him."

"I once heard from Prince Arnold that his father ordered him to marry someone with royal blood from another country."

Rishe herself had blood ties to her country's royal family. Distant ties, but they were enough for Arnold's father to approve of their union. *If I learn about his mother, maybe I'll understand a little more about why Prince Arnold proposed to me.* Or perhaps she was being naive.

I have no idea if figuring that out will lead to avoiding the war in the next few years. I still feel like it's more important to investigate the coup d'état that starts the war—Prince Arnold's murder of his father, the current emperor. There's one other thing...

While Rishe was deliberating, Theodore stretched and stood up with a yawn. "Guess I should head back."

"I'm sorry for interrupting your rest."

"You'd better be! I wouldn't trade an opportunity to talk about my brother for anything else, though, so it's fine. Ah, what time is it?"

"From the position of the sun, I'd say three hours past noon."

Theodore was taken aback by Rishe's swift answer. "I'd prefer if you announced the time after hearing a church bell or looking at a clock, you know."

"It's just a guess, so it's not as accurate as a clock. Come to think of it, Prince Theodore..." She wanted to ask her future brother-in-law something she'd been wondering for a long time now, something she'd asked Arnold too. "Down there, in the town, there's a beautiful spire. What *is* that?"

Theodore glanced at the tower and replied, "It's a church. The second biggest and most impressive on the continent, apparently, so even foreigners travel to worship there. They pray together once a month and sing together once a year. It's a pretty important building, I guess."

"I see..." It seemed there really was something that needed her confirmation. Rishe's gaze dropped as she formulated a plan.

She thanked Theodore, parted with him, and met up with her waiting guards nearby. Then she headed back to the detached palace, whereupon she visited Arnold's office and asked to speak to him alone.

Taking her place on the couch opposite him, she put one hand on top of the other on her lap. "Prince Arnold."

"Yes? What's with the solemn look?"

"Well, I'm here with a rather selfish request." Arnold urged her to continue with his eyes, so Rishe said flatly, "I'd like to officially annul my engagement."

He said nothing, watching her.

"Oh, of course I mean my—"

Arnold stood before Rishe could finish and sat down beside her, eyes fixed on her all the while. Rishe gulped as he said, "If that is your wish..."

"Yes?" She hadn't finished explaining, but Arnold hadn't asked her to. *It's Prince Arnold we're talking about. I'm sure he's already predicted my thoughts and knows exactly what I want to say.*

Arnold's shapely hands reached out and combed through her coral-colored hair.

"Eep!"

Ever since Rishe told Arnold he could touch her directly a few days ago, he'd developed a habit of stroking her hair. He tended to touch her just next to her ear, which tickled and made her feel anxious in a strange way. Arnold probably felt like he was petting an animal, but Rishe was always caught unawares by his touch. The surprise was bad for her heart. And to make it all worse, his face was so close to hers; she felt cornered.

"Y-Your Highness?"

The most beautiful man in the world (as far as Rishe was aware) whispered to her in a low voice, "I'll have to interfere with whatever method I can."

"Huh?" Rishe was speechless for a moment. She wondered why he would say something like that and then realized there had been a misunderstanding. "W-wait a second! I wasn't clear enough. Let me finish what I was saying! Please back up a bit!"

"No. You just said you wanted to annul your engagement, didn't you?"

"I did, but I didn't! I have no intention of fleeing from whatever your scheme is! The engagement I want to officially annul is...!"

My previous engagement with Dietrich.

When she explained herself, Arnold furrowed his brow deeply and heaved a sigh.

***

The crown prince of Galkhein's personal carriage headed south down the highway.

It feels like we came this far in the blink of an eye.

Another half a day of travel and their destination would come into view. Rishe had donned a cool dress the color of new leaves to match the coming summer season. She glanced across the carriage at Arnold, who was reading some documents.

I'm really surprised. I didn't think Prince Arnold would accompany me all this way.

Rishe recalled the conversation she'd had with Arnold a week ago.

"What I mean to say is, my childhood engagement with Prince Dietrich hasn't been officially annulled yet," Rishe told Arnold in his office.

At last, Arnold understood her meaning. "You performed an engagement ceremony with the crown prince of Hermity."

"Yes, exactly. Though it's a very old ceremony, so no royal families still hold them."

An engagement ceremony was different from a marriage ceremony. Most of them were political affairs held while the betrothed were children. Since these contracts were often established years before the actual wedding, the engagement ceremony served to make the engagements harder to break. It hadn't stopped Dietrich, however.

"It was something my parents requested of the Hermity royal family."

Rishe had only the faintest memory of the event. All she remembered was getting roused from her sleep early and dressed, the exhaustion hanging over her the whole time, and Dietrich being wound up because of the atypical situation they were in.

"So, your engagement with that man is still registered with the Church."

"It was a shock to me too. The engagement ceremony is rare as it is, and there aren't many instances of annulling them in the past." Rishe closed her eyes and nodded gravely. "I completely forgot that I can't marry another man without going to the Grand Basilica to officially annul my previous engagement!"

Of course, this was a complete lie. Rishe was well aware that she had to file an annulment of her engagement with Dietrich at the Grand Basilica if she wanted to marry another man. She'd had an occasion to visit the Grand Basilica in her fourth life, and a bishop there had told her just that. She'd hastily filed for the annulment right then and there.

I knew I would have to in this life too, but I came to Galkhein without doing it on purpose... I wanted to give myself an opportunity to escape through my engagement to Prince Dietrich if I decided I didn't want to marry Prince Arnold.

The ceremony wasn't performed in most countries, so she figured Arnold wouldn't be aware of this. Rishe regarded Arnold through her downcast eyelashes. *I think I'm okay at this point, though. I don't see myself itching to get out of marrying Prince Arnold. After all, he's kind, and nice, and considerate...*

"What is it?"

"Oh! Nothing!"

Since she had the convenient engagement, she figured it would be a waste to annul it without using this opportunity to further her goals—so she took it upon herself to do a little investigating.

I've always been curious about Prince Arnold's relationship with the Crusade.

It was said that this world once had a goddess. A religion called the Crusade revered this goddess and created the calendar, along with various religious teachings. These teachings were spread and believed worldwide. Rishe's homeland and Galkhein were no exception. There were differing levels of faith among the people, but the teachings influenced almost everyone to some extent. Spouses vowed their love to the goddess at weddings, and families celebrated the goddess's birthday together.

Most nobles had, in addition to their first and last names, a baptismal name they'd received from the Church—so ubiquitous was the Crusade and the goddess's teaching that this practice was common everywhere. Rishe's own middle name, Irmgard, was her baptismal name.

Galkhein is one of the most powerful countries in the world. But as powerful as Galkhein is, the Crusade is about as powerful, and it's been around for a lot longer.

However, one man's hand would turn that major religion to ash.

Five years from now, Prince Arnold—by then, Emperor Arnold—will burn the Church to the ground. He set fire to every church he could find, dragged their bishops before their adherents, and killed them. He torched every bible and faith symbol he could find too, until not a single trace remained. I saw it once with my own eyes.

Before this life, she'd thought Arnold's motivation was just the destruction of a large, powerful organization. But something had been bothering her for a while now since she'd gotten to know him in this life.

You can see down into Galkhein's castle town from the detached palace. The first day I came to the palace, I asked Prince Arnold what the large spire in the east of the town was, and...

Arnold had said, *"The church and clock tower. The bells ring out the hour."* From what Theodore told her, however, she knew something about Arnold's answer was off.

Prince Arnold hardly mentioned the church. He was only concerned about the tower's function as a clock.

That stuck in her mind, given that she was aware of Arnold's future actions.

It's weird for him to mention only that when speaking of a church. You'd think he would mention the church's authority or political value, like his brother did. He must've deliberately avoided talking about it.

Maybe Arnold harbored hidden feelings toward the Crusade. If those feelings were connected to the violence he'd perpetrate in five years, then Rishe had ample reason to find out and prevent it.

Plus, this is my only opportunity to meet you-know-who in this life… That said, I'll have to come up with a natural-sounding excuse if I want to get close to the Grand Basilica for my investigation.

Annulling her engagement with Dietrich was the perfect chance. She'd come up with this idea just the other day after receiving a letter. Rishe took the letter out and showed it to Arnold. "Lady Mary, Prince Dietrich's current partner, worked hard to get him to annul the engagement on his end. It's very difficult to do so, but Lady Mary came forward as Prince Dietrich's partner in infidelity, which made the process much easier."

Arnold languidly regarded the letter in Rishe's hands.

"It says the process is complete on Prince Dietrich's side of things, so all I need to do is finalize it at the Grand Basilica. I won't have to see him as part of the process, so I think I'll get it done quickly."

"…"

"I apologize for the abruptness of the matter, but would it be all right if I headed to the Grand Basilica in the Holy Kingdom of Domana sometime in the next few days? If I hurry, I can probably make it back in about a week."

Although she framed it as a question, Arnold had no choice but to let her go. After all, if Rishe didn't go to the Grand Basilica, she wouldn't be able to marry someone aside from Dietrich. She didn't know what Arnold's grand plan was, but as long as it involved their marriage, she was confident he would permit her to go.

I'd really like Prince Arnold to come along too, honestly, Rishe thought, watching Arnold frown. After all, the whole point of this voyage was to probe into Arnold's feelings toward the Church. If the man himself accompanied her, it would undoubtedly be easier to find that out.

He has his hands full, though. I'm sure it won't work out. I had to rush through my preparations for the marriage ceremony just to give myself enough time to leave.

But as she was telling herself that it wouldn't work out...

"I'll accompany you, then."

"Huh?!" she exclaimed, not expecting to hear that.

Arnold was still sitting next to her. Calm as still water, he asked, "What? Is that inconvenient for you?"

Exactly the opposite, in fact! Things were *too* convenient, hence her shock.

While she was trying to puzzle out his motives, Arnold put his arm up on the back of the couch and explained, "I have several duties related to the Church that I've neglected. I put them off because I didn't want to bother, but if I can go in person and get them all taken care of at once, then this is a perfect opportunity."

That's probably a lie...

"Plus..." Arnold paused, and Rishe cocked her head, waiting for him to continue. Eventually, he just said, "No. It's nothing."

This was rare. She could hardly remember another instance of Arnold taking back his words. He really did act odd over matters pertaining to the Church.

Then again, I could just be imagining it. I wonder what's going on here?

She stared hard at him, but it wasn't like that allowed her to read his thoughts. If she wanted to get a sense of what he was thinking, the best thing would be for him to accompany her.

A few days later, their carriage departed for the Holy Kingdom of Domana. Several days after that, they made it to their current location.

I didn't really expect him to come with me, Rishe thought as their carriage headed for the Grand Basilica.

Arnold sat across from her, sorting through paperwork in silence. She was worried about him feeling sick, but he wore the same cool expression for the whole ride. The stack of documents at his side had been handed to him by his attendant, Oliver, who looked like he was on death's door. There was a second stack just like it in another carriage.

Rishe apologized to Oliver in her mind as she organized the medicinal herbs she'd been able to find on the road. *Well, it is pretty reckless for the crown prince to leave the country for a week with no warning! I'm sorry, Oliver, but because Prince Arnold is with us, we can change horses at regular intervals. We're making great time on our way to the Grand Basilica!*

"Galkhein always impresses me," Rishe said as she separated

the sepals from a flower that could be used to create an antidote. "The road all the way to the Grand Basilica has been maintained very well. If it weren't, I don't think this trip would have been this smooth even though Domana neighbors Galkhein."

The jostling vibrations of a carriage made long rides exhausting. Paved roads significantly eased the burden of travel.

Arnold turned a page in his documents with an indifferent expression and said, "A hefty budget goes to maintaining this road. We get good tax yields from the towns along the highway, since so many people go to the Grand Basilica to worship."

"Long-distance travel moves a lot of money. Though, if there's so much traffic, that must mean there are a lot of devout believers in Galkhein, huh? The Church allows only the highway from Galkhein to come near the Grand Basilica too."

That was another thing Rishe was curious about. The power dynamic between Galkhein and the Church was something no two other powers in the world shared. The Church had power surpassing that of a nation. As such, they had no reason to give favorable treatment to any powerful domains or their royal families. What set the Church apart was their *own* royal line, which was said to have inherited the blood of the goddess.

The Church's relationship with Galkhein stood out from the rest; Galkhein having the second-biggest church in the world was evidence of that. They were the same size everywhere else so as not to suggest any disparity between countries' ties to the Church.

It's not just that the Church treats Galkhein differently. Galkhein hasn't invaded the Holy Kingdom either.

The reason Domana neighbored Galkhein was that Galkhein had absorbed all the other countries between them in the last war.

Even though the Holy Kingdom doesn't have a strong military, Galkhein still allows it to exist to their south without threat of invasion.

Arnold's father had been very aggressive about starting wars. Arnold painted him as a belligerent man too. So why had he left a country alone that was politically important but militarily weak?

In my merchant loop, the rumor I heard all around the world was that Galkhein's emperor was very devout. If that's the case, did Prince Arnold burn churches to antagonize his father?

Opposite her, Arnold lifted his gaze from a page to peer at her. "More importantly, was it really all right not to bring any of your maids with you?"

"Yes. Only a select few can enter the Grand Basilica at the moment. If they had to wait in a nearby town for the duration of our visit, it makes more sense for them to remain in the detached palace instead."

"All thanks to that festival. This trip is occurring at quite an inconvenient time."

Actually, we're here now precisely because *they're preparing for the festival, but I can't tell him that!*

The carriage gradually slowed. Rishe looked out the window, but they were passing through a forest on the highway. They were neither at their destination nor at a rest stop, yet the vehicle came to a halt. Rishe sensed Arnold starting to rise and grabbed his sleeve.

He frowned at her. "Something's not right. Stay in the carriage."

"I'm not letting you leave me in here a second time. Also, you should be well aware that locking the door is pointless, Your Highness."

This was the second time she'd gotten into an unusual situation on a carriage trip with Arnold. Last time, Arnold had gotten the better of her—but not this time.

Arnold sighed and got out first, then held out his hand to Rishe. She smiled, took his hand, and stepped down from the carriage. Their guards' carriage up ahead had stopped. The knights who had disembarked were standing around looking perplexed.

"What happened?" Arnold asked them.

"Your Highness! Well, a carriage from another country is blocking the road."

Rishe had a hunch when she heard that report. *It couldn't be...* A certain someone came to mind—and at almost the exact same moment, Rishe heard her.

"I don't want it! I hate it, I hate it, I don't *want* it!" A young girl's clear, animated voice echoed through the nearby trees.

Arnold glanced in the direction of the sound. The door to a pure-white carriage opened, and a girl who looked about ten years old flew out of it.

"Will you be reasonable?! What do you hate about it?! You specifically said you wanted a white carriage, and you were perfectly happy riding in it a moment ago!"

"I changed my mind! Now I want a black carriage! I want it! And if I can't have it—"

It was then that the girl locked eyes with Rishe's party. She was pretty in a doll-like way, with big, bright eyes. Her long violet hair fell in gentle waves down her back. Her frilly, lemon-colored dress made her look a little immature for her age but suited her adorable appearance quite well. A polished pair of shoes topped it all off.

When the girl noticed that Rishe and Arnold's carriage was black, she screwed up her face with resolute courage and shouted, "I've decided! If you won't listen to me, Papa, then..." She sprinted over to them and grabbed Rishe's skirt. "I'll ride in these people's carriage!"

"Millia! Don't cause trouble to strangers!"

Ah, yes... Rishe regarded the girl and suppressed a sigh. *I see you haven't changed, Mistress Millia.*

This girl was the noble lady Rishe had served in her fourth loop—and the whole reason Rishe had set off on this trip.

***

In her fourth life, a year and a half from the present, Rishe became Lady Millia Clarissa Jonal's maid. She had been working for a marquess in Domana, getting along well with the young, rowdy sons of the family, and had received a request to do the same sort of work for the Jonal family. She'd headed to the family home, where she'd met the eleven-year-old Millia.

Millia was a very moody child. The other maids kept their distance from her as a result. An old illness had left her father—

the duke—partially paralyzed, and he was prone to bouts of ill health. Since he couldn't be with his daughter as much as he wanted, he tended to spoil her to keep her happy. As a result, she'd developed a selfish streak that he could no longer control.

When Rishe arrived at their house, the first thing the head maid told her was *"You watch out for Mistress Millia too. She's very difficult to handle, a real problem child."*

But...

Meeting Millia for the first time again in her seventh life, Rishe looked down at the crown of the girl's head as she clung to her waist.

A man in his forties who looked to be at the end of his rope climbed down from Millia's carriage. "Millia, you're bothering them!"

Duke Jonal.

The noble hurried over. He had combed-back blond hair and a tidy mustache. He was Rishe's former master, though he didn't have the walking cane Rishe remembered.

I heard that Duke Jonal was paralyzed by an illness he'd suffered a long time ago, but...

Apparently, the condition hadn't taken him just yet.

He walked up to Rishe and offered her a polite bow. "I'm terribly sorry for my daughter's behavior, Miss. Let go of her, Millia!"

"No! Nooo!" Millia screamed with all her might and tightened her grip. She buried her face in Rishe's skirts, though Rishe was a complete stranger to her now.

"Millia!"

"I hate you, Papa! You won't do what I ask, and you scold me about it too! I'm only bothering these people because you're being mean to me!" Millia shouted.

Arnold scowled. Rishe noticed him about to move and signaled him not to with her eyes. She looked down at Millia again and said to her, "Young lady—"

"Don't talk to me! You're just going to take Papa's side, aren't you?! Even though we just met and you don't know what's going on and you haven't heard my side of it!"

"Do you think you could look up at me, young lady?"

"Wh-why? What do you want?!" Millia's head angrily shot up...and she gasped.

Rishe spread out a white lace handkerchief. Millia watched her, puzzled. Taking advantage of that second of confusion, Rishe balled up the handkerchief in her right hand. She put that fist on top of her left hand, tapped it, and then opened both hands after a beat.

"Huh?!"

The handkerchief had disappeared without a trace. Instead, it had been replaced by a small stuffed bear. A buzz went through the watching servants and knights, but Millia, who had been watching up close, was the most surprised of all.

"M-m-magic?!" Millia's cheeks flushed red, and her eyes sparkled.

Rishe beamed at her. "No, young lady. A magic *trick*. Here, to commemorate our meeting."

"I can have it?!"

"Of course."

Rishe offered her the stuffed bear, and the girl's clenched hands began to relax. Crouching down to Millia's level, Rishe introduced herself. "My name is Rishe Irmgard Weitzner. What's your name, young lady?"

"I'm Millia Clarissa Jonal. I'm Papa's daughter, and I'm almost ten."

"Lady Millia, then." She couldn't exactly call her "Mistress" in this life. Feeling a bit sad about that, Rishe handed Millia the stuffed animal she'd prepared for their meeting. "I hope you like it."

Shrinking in on herself with a little grunt, Millia shyly wrapped her hands around the bear and looked away from Rishe. "Um, thank you."

Jonal looked on in disbelief. "My word... I never expected Millia to act so meek."

You see, Your Grace, Mistress Millia is actually a good girl with a pure heart.

After meeting the eleven-year-old Millia and being charged with her care, Rishe had learned the young girl was more childlike than her age would suggest. They had cultivated flowers together, gone on walks in the forest, and slept in the same bed on stormy nights. Since Millia didn't like studying, Rishe spent many hours reading the textbooks with her. And when Millia turned fifteen—the age Rishe was now—she became a happy bride.

But that day... Rishe stood and closed her eyes. *Right after Mistress Millia's wedding ceremony, Galkhein's military stormed the church.*

And Rishe had been killed.

Although she had been a maid, Rishe was like an older sister to Millia and had thus been allowed to attend the ceremony. She was in the church when Galkhein's soldiers invaded. She had lived just long enough to see Millia and her family evacuated from the burning building.

I wonder if Prince Arnold was there in that church where I died. Curious, Rishe snuck a peek at Arnold. He seemed to have been watching her exchange with Millia dispassionately, but his gaze met Rishe's. *I'm sure he was.* Arnold had given the order as well. It was by his will that that beautiful church was burned down, killing the people inside.

Rishe lowered her gaze and took a deep, furtive breath. Then she raised her head and called her fiancé's name. "Prince Arnold." She walked over to him and protested in a low voice, "You were staring right at me when I did that magic trick!"

Arnold averted his gaze and replied, "What was I supposed to do? You were leading everyone to pay attention to your right hand, but your left hand was making clearly unnatural movements."

"Most people focus on the right hand like they're supposed to! Even if you noticed it, you should go along with the act!"

"That trick requires you to hide something in your dress sleeve. You're awfully well prepared, aren't you?"

Rishe was tempted to look away, but she didn't want him suspecting her, so she mustered her boldness and faced him instead. "Actually, I was planning on showing it to you once we had a rest on our journey."

"Oh? You're really telling me you were going to pull a stuffed bear out for me?"

"I-It's so fluffy, I thought it would relax you, Your Highness..."

"Hah!" Arnold barked out a laugh. Rishe's eyes nearly popped out at the surprisingly open gesture. "Well, so be it. We can go with that."

"Ugh! The truth is that I was practicing in case there were small children at the Basilica!"

"I see. That's too bad."

She didn't know what was "too bad," but she decided to drop it. If she didn't, Arnold would grow even more suspicious.

It was a way for me to interact with Mistress Millia if we encountered her at the Grand Basilica or on the road. I doubt Prince Arnold thinks I intended to run into Mistress Millia from the beginning... The problem is what she and her father believe.

Rishe turned around and observed the father and daughter, who were much calmer than they had been earlier.

"Please be good, Millia. It's only a little bit farther to the Grand Basilica. You can ride in a white carriage, can't you?"

"Well, now that I look at it, white is childish, isn't it?! I was chosen to stand in for the royal priestess in the festival, so I need to ride in a carriage that suits my role!"

The servants and maids of the Jonal family watched the exchange with anxious expressions. Rishe didn't recognize a face among them.

This is all too strange.

Something about the situation bothered her.

Mistress Millia was never this *spoiled. Sure, she complained about studying and whined about wanting sweets, but she was never so unreasonable about concrete things like the color of her carriage. I suppose it's possible she was this way before I met her at eleven, but...*

She side-eyed Duke Jonal as well. She'd always heard that he had been unwell for a long time, but the man before her now was the very picture of health. Maybe he looked a little tired, but that made sense for someone dealing with a difficult daughter's temper tantrums in close quarters.

The duke sighed deeply and turned back to Rishe and Arnold with a bow. "I apologize for the late introduction. I am Josef Ehrenfried Jonal. I have the honor of serving as a duke in the Holy Kingdom of Domana. I apologize for my daughter's behavior." His eyes flicked to the crest of Galkhein on Arnold's carriage. "I don't suppose you two belong to the royal family of Galkhein?"

Arnold took a short breath and introduced himself as the crown prince. "I'm Arnold Hein. I'm sure you're familiar with my father, the emperor."

Jonal gasped softly. He hid his agitation well, but Rishe—and likely Arnold—had picked up on it right away. Covering it up with a smile, he said, "So, I have the honor of speaking to His Highness the crown prince. This young lady must be your new fiancée. Once again, I am so very sorry for my daughter's rudeness."

"Well, if it hasn't bothered my wife..."

"Of course not. I appreciate the opportunity to meet such an adorable young lady," Rishe said. While Arnold and Duke Jonal were exchanging pleasantries, Rishe knelt and approached Millia with a gentle smile. "Lady Millia, why do you fight with your father?"

"I'm the stand-in for the late royal priestess, but my papa doesn't understand that. The festival is almost here, so I must play my part perfectly or I'll embarrass the goddess and the real royal priestess!"

"My! So, you'll be serving as the royal priestess in the next festival, Lady Millia?"

Rishe knew all this, but she acted like she was hearing it for the first time. The Crusade held a festival to celebrate the goddess, the central figure of their faith. Normally, a priestess said to have the blood of the goddess appeared at the festival as her proxy and offered up a prayer. The Church had protected these women for generations—until the last royal priestess died in an accident twenty-two years ago. Men carried on the bloodline, but only a woman could perform the role of the royal priestess.

That's why the Church hasn't held the festival for two decades. But after all the complaints from the faithful, they're going to start doing festivals with a stand-in royal priestess this year.

She thought back on the explanation she'd heard in her fourth loop. "If I recall correctly, only a noble lady from a house in the Holy Kingdom of Domana can serve as the royal priestess's stand-in. You were chosen for that position, Lady Millia?"

"That's right! It's a great honor, you know. But Papa..." Millia pressed her lips in a tight line, then muttered, "Papa's stupid. Making me mad..."

Rishe blinked. She had never heard Millia speak so quietly before. Up until just a moment ago, Millia had been throwing a temper tantrum as if she were a much younger child. Now she looked to be beyond her years as she watched her father.

"Even though I could curse him, he still doesn't believe that everyone I curse dies."

A chill crept up Rishe's spine, and she shuddered. "Lady Millia, what are you...?" She trailed off, unable to muster more. An expression she'd never seen before had etched itself on the face of her once-mistress.

When she thought about it, she *did* recall a conversation they'd had one night when they were sleeping in the same bed.

"You know, Rishe, I once had a power I had to keep secret. I can't use it anymore, and I promised Papa I'd never tell anyone what kind of power it was...but it's true."

Millia was a simple and headstrong girl, but during that conversation, her face had clouded—very unusual. Thinking about it now, Rishe imagined that the uneasy expression she'd worn then might have something to do with this "curse" she'd mentioned.

There's no such thing as magic or curses...is what someone normal would probably be thinking right about now. Rishe, however, couldn't dismiss the possibility, as she herself was reliving her life due to some mysterious power.

While she contemplated what to say to Millia, she felt a prick on the back of her neck. It was just for a second, and it was likely no one else had noticed it, but she knew what it was as she turned around.

Prince Arnold?

Arnold seemed to have finished exchanging pleasantries with the duke and was staring her way. More precisely, he was scrutinizing Millia with an awfully cold look in his eyes. It was not the sort of look one gave a young girl upon meeting her for the first time.

Those icy eyes reminded Rishe of someone. *That's the same look in the emperor Arnold Hein's eyes five years from now.*

Arnold, who would burn churches to the ground in the future, approached the stand-in royal priestess. Rishe reflexively turned to Millia, but the girl didn't seem to even notice Arnold looking at her.

"I'll go back to my carriage now. Th-thank you for the stuffed animal!"

"Oh, Lady Millia...!"

The girl skittered off and disappeared into her carriage. Her father gave a deep bow of his head to Rishe, who curtsied in response and then sucked in a breath.

"Rishe, we're leaving. Come here."

"Yes, Your Highness."

Arnold had returned to his usual expressionless state. At his call, Rishe followed him to the carriage and returned to her seat. She looked out the window and found the duke and his entourage waiting on either side of the road. They may have had the royal priestess's stand-in on board, but they still represented a duke. They likely intended to wait a while before departing so as not to crowd the carriages of another country's royals.

I guess we'll be arriving at the Grand Basilica first, then. Rishe glanced at Arnold. *That look he gave her... Prince Arnold hasn't noticed you-know-what, has he?* She frowned, recalling something about Duke Jonal's family. *It couldn't be... No, I should ask about it. I can be direct here.*

Rishe studied Arnold the whole time she was thinking. When the carriage began moving again and Arnold picked up his paperwork, he asked, "What?"

"You were giving Lady Millia an awfully frightening glare earlier."

Arnold looked up at her from his papers; he must not have expected her to be so forthright. "I didn't think I was looking at her any differently than I normally would."

"Well, you were. You usually have a gentler look on your face, Your Highness."

"..."

She was taken aback when Arnold scowled then—she hadn't expected a frown until later in the conversation. "Huh? Is something wrong?"

"You're just about the only person who'd say something like that about me."

"I don't think that's true."

"Whatever."

Rishe tilted her head, and Arnold set his documents down next to him. He propped his elbow on the window frame and put his chin in his hand while lowering his eyes.

"There was no particular reason for it. I just don't like children."

I see. So that's what he's going with. Rishe decided to push a little harder. "Still, Lady Millia's already almost ten. Isn't your third sister about that age, Prince Arnold?"

"I don't care and I don't remember."

I wonder if he means that, Rishe thought, unconvinced. She couldn't exactly take him at his word considering the difference in how he felt versus how he acted toward Theodore.

Her skepticism was plain on her face, so Arnold sighed and, still expressionless, told her, "I don't believe in unconditional love between family members. Blood ties have nothing to do with how well two people get along."

"I suppose you have a point." Rishe didn't have a great relationship with her parents either. If Arnold considered his family to be more like strangers, then she didn't really have an argument against him. *Why do I feel like he was referring to his father more so than his sister, though?*

Arnold's gaze was fixed on something in the distance. Rishe followed his line of sight and spotted a resplendent stone building: the Grand Basilica. This same building would've probably been nothing but ashes after Rishe's death.

We'll only be able to stay there for a few days. I have to finish my investigation before the annulment's finalized.

About an hour later, their carriage arrived at the Grand Basilica. Arnold took Rishe's hand once more, and they stepped out of the carriage.

That was when it happened.

"Stop! Hey, what are you doing?!"

They heard a knight shouting behind them and the neighing of a horse. Rishe whirled around just in time to see a boy of about ten years toppling off a horse to the ground. The boy's shoulders heaved with each breath he took; he must have been exhausted. Arnold's imperial guards surrounded the boy out of both caution and concern. Rishe wanted to rush over as well, but Arnold had her wrist tight in his grip.

She could tell at a glance that this was an unusual situation. *The crest on the horse's saddle is that of Duke Jonal's family. What's going on here?*

Rishe got a glimpse of the boy and gasped.

I know him!

In her sixth loop, there was a boy Rishe had always looked out for. He was four years younger than her, so he would be eleven now. He had glossy brown hair and a cherubic face, but he also had a habit of giving adults dirty looks. The black eyepatch covering one of his eyes didn't exactly soften his impression.

The boy who'd fallen off the horse looked just like him. There was always a possibility that she was wrong, but the resemblance was uncanny. He looked shorter than she remembered him, but since she was meeting him six months earlier than she had the first time, that made sense. *I never heard anything about this, though.*

He looked up at the knights and, through ragged breaths, barely managed to squeeze out the words, "Please...help..."

"Take it easy. Can you speak? Go slow if you need to."

"The...duke..."

"Just breathe. Somebody, bring some water!"

"Prince Arnold, please let me go!" Rishe said, and Arnold released his grip on her. But before she could make her way to the knights, he stepped in front of her and knelt before the boy himself.

The knights tried to stop him. "Your Highness! Please step back. He may be a child, but you could still be in danger..."

"If you can't speak, nod or shake your head. Did something happen to Lord Jonal?"

The boy nodded, and Rishe felt her heart throb with anxiety.

"Is the duke already dead?"

The boy shook his head furiously.

"Then, is his life still in danger now?"

The boy shook his head again. Rishe relaxed for a second before going pale at Arnold's next question.

"Does the same go for his daughter?"

The boy nodded.

Oh, thank goodness...

Arnold narrowed his eyes and stood back up. They had at least determined that the situation wasn't *so* dire. One of the knights brought the boy a cup of water and supported his back as he drank from it. He took a shaky breath after downing the water.

"If you can speak now, explain the situation."

"Th-their carriage..." When he finally managed to speak, Rishe heard just the voice she'd been expecting to hear. He really was Leo, the boy she'd known. Looking like he was about to cry, Leo added, "It suddenly lost a wheel!"

What?

"Lord Jonal jumped out of the carriage with Lady Millia in his arms. But the carriage and horses fell into a valley, and Master hurt his arm."

Millia's voice replayed in Rishe's mind: *"We're going to the Grand Basilica, but I don't want to ride in this childish carriage. But Papa doesn't understand..."*

"Even though I could curse him, he still doesn't believe that everyone I curse dies."

After Millia had thrown her fit, the carriage she complained about had fallen into a pit—and the duke, who'd scolded her, had gotten injured. It was like the "curse" Millia spoke of had become real.

Rishe found herself gripping her dress. *What is going on?*

CHAPTER 2

WHEN RISHE JOINED the order of knights in her sixth life, Leo had been assigned to do chores there while wounds all over his body were healing. Leo was the prickly sort, but he mostly kept to himself and did good work. He was always hanging his head, displaying his long and unkempt hair. Rishe had known him for years but had never really gotten him to open up to her.

Just once, she saw what was under his eyepatch. His eye was sealed fully shut by a painful-looking scar. It was obvious at a glance that the injury had been a serious one.

One day, Rishe asked a senior knight she bunked with, "Joel, do you know how Leo joined the knights?"

"Hmm?" Encamped in the upper bunk of their bed, her senior spent his free time sleeping. Today was a rare day when he was actually awake. He lazily raised his head and peered at Rishe, who was sitting in a chair against the wall. Then he called her by the nickname of Lucius, Rishe's male knight persona. "Lu, are you trying to stick your nose into other people's business again?"

"N-no, it's just...today, after finishing his duties, he sat all alone in a corner of the training grounds and watched everyone else practice again."

Joel narrowed his already sleepy eyes. "Hmm? So, you could afford to be distracted when you can't even beat me, huh? How cheeky."

"How could I when you were napping on a bench?!"

Her senior just yawned, unconcerned, and then turned over. Still, he didn't completely abandon the conversation. "They found him in a ship's hold. Our lord, who happened to be there, took him in. The little guy told his story while he was feverish from festering wounds. Something about how he screwed up big time at his last job. He was beaten for it so bad, he thought he was gonna die. So he fled."

"An eleven-year-old child was severely punished just for making a mistake at his job?"

"Rich people who treat their employees inhumanely aren't that rare. Look, I only told you 'cause I know you're not gonna blab about it, all right? Don't try to dig any deeper," Joel said, covering himself with his blanket again. "Leo's stuck with those nasty wounds of his unless you find some way to turn back time."

***

There was a soft knock on the door to the anteroom in the Grand Basilica.

"Pardon me, Your Highness, Lady Rishe."

Oliver, Arnold's attendant, entered the room. He approached the couch where Arnold sat, swiftly bowed, and reported, "His Grace Jonal and his daughter have retired to their room. He expressed his desire to formally thank you for allowing them to borrow your carriage."

"Tell him there's no need. Any change in the duke's or his daughter's condition?"

"The lady was only crying from the shock of the carriage's fall. She finally calmed down just a minute ago."

Arnold turned to Rishe, who sat beside him. "So he says."

He'd inquired about their conditions not out of personal concern but for Rishe's sake.

"Thank you..." Rishe sighed and relaxed her muscles. *I'm glad to hear it.*

Arnold and Rishe had sprung into action after hearing about the accident. With Leo's guidance, they'd headed to the site of the accident and helped the duke and Millia, who were trembling by the roadside, into their own carriage. Rishe had also quickly examined them to check for injuries. Afterward, their knights went to retrieve the fallen carriage. Thankfully, the horses hadn't been fatally injured, but the carriage had crashed into a tree on the way down and taken serious damage.

Millia had bawled and clung to Rishe the whole way back. A chagrined Duke Jonal—who'd bruised an arm—tried to soothe his daughter and thanked Rishe and Arnold again and again. When he saw the boy sitting stiff in the carriage, he also said, "Thank you for going and getting help, Leo."

After all that, Rishe and Arnold had made their way back to the Grand Basilica.

I do hope Mistress Millia is getting some rest in her room. I've got more important things to consider, though.

Rishe had a new concern. *Lord Jonal called that boy "Leo." He* must *be the Leo I know. But he's not wearing an eyepatch, and his left eye is perfectly fine. Hmm...*

Evidently, whatever events led to the boy losing an eye had yet to occur.

Joel told me Leo was battered by his previous employer. Leo ends up with the knights three months from now. Considering the timing, that would mean his "previous employer" is Duke Jonal.

At this, she dropped her gaze to the floor.

I never heard anything about His Grace beating his servants. He was always the sort of person who forgave new workers' mistakes with a warm smile. It's hard to imagine him giving such a terrible beating to an eleven-year-old child.

However, since there are no servants here, I assume there will be a big change in his staff soon—and there must be a reason for it. Then there's this "curse" Mistress Millia mentioned...

Each new thought that occurred to her was worse than the last.

Maybe the curse really does exist.

She lowered her head discreetly so as not to catch Arnold's eye.

What if Leo's injuries weren't caused by Duke Jonal but by someone else he was trying to cover for? And to hide what happened, maybe he dismissed all the servants who knew about it. The only one Lord Jonal would go so far to protect is...

Rishe looked up at Arnold. "It's true we don't need their thanks, but I would at least like to see them once they recover."

"..."

"I'm worried about that boy who came to get us too. He must have pushed himself hard to get to us as quickly as he did."

The prince stared back at Rishe with open displeasure. Eventually, though, he sighed and said, "Oliver, schedule something."

"Very well. Thank you for persuading His Highness, Lady Rishe."

Just my own personal motives here, unfortunately.

Before long, there was another knock at the door. This time, it was a young priest.

"Your Highness, the archbishop will see you now."

Arnold said nothing in response, but...

He's scowling so blatantly!

He and Rishe had different appointments for the simple reason that they had different errands. Arnold was here on official political business with the Church, and Rishe was just trying to annul her engagement with Prince Dietrich. Arnold would be speaking to the archbishop, one of the leaders of the Church. Rishe, on the other hand, could meet with any bishop with a certain level of authority. As such, the two of them would be parting ways for a time.

"Um, Prince Arnold, the priest is waiting for you."

Arnold clicked his tongue in frustration and flicked his eyes up to Oliver, who stood at his side. "Oliver, I want you to stay with Rishe."

Oliver put a hand to his heart and bowed. "As you wish."

At last, Arnold stood and left the room with the priest. The door closed, and Rishe was left alone with Oliver.

"Ah, this really helps!" Oliver said with a smile, looking refreshed. "When you're around, my lord becomes so much more reasonable. I wish he were always like this."

"Reasonable," Oliver? Really?

Oliver spoke about Arnold as if he were a child, but he'd been serving the man for ten years. That meant he'd become Arnold's attendant when Arnold was nine. If he had been serving at Arnold's side for that long, maybe speaking about his lord in that manner was only natural.

"Well, really, I know that I need to be able to persuade him without you, Lady Rishe. I'm honestly embarrassed by my incompetence."

"You're not incompetent, Oliver. Besides, I'm sure His Highness only acts so spoiled with you *because* it's you he's dealing with. It's proof that he trusts you."

If they were so close, Rishe hoped Arnold had told him the reason he'd proposed to her—although even if he had, there was no guarantee that Oliver would tell her. As she thought this, Oliver's smile turned warm.

"You really do keep a close eye on my lord, don't you, Lady Rishe?"

Oh... Rishe had known people who smiled like that in the past. It was the same smile Rishe's fellow knights had worn when they spoke of the king they served: loyal, proud, respectful, and affectionate all at once. *They have a very solid relationship. I hope I can ask Oliver about Prince Arnold one day.*

If she wasn't smart about how she asked, however, she could envision the question making its way back to Arnold. Rishe decided to start with a roundabout, indirect line of questioning.

"Have you always been so close with Prince Arnold, Oliver?"

"Ha ha ha, of course not." Oliver laughed, amused, still wearing that refreshing smile. "We first met just after my lord killed all of his servants at the age of nine."

Rishe couldn't believe her ears.

Oliver ignored her shocked silence and continued nonchalantly, "I wasn't exactly the most devoted attendant back then, either, having just been injured and forced to abandon my life as a knight. I was disowned by my family, so I was more or less looking for a place to die when I began serving my lord."

"..."

"Oh. Have you not heard of the incident?" he asked, and Rishe shook her head vigorously. Oliver gave a thoughtful hum. "There must be far fewer rumors going around the palace now, then. I'll have to put a couple more into circulation."

As Rishe stood there, stock-still, the third knock of the day occurred.

"That must be your escort, Lady Rishe. Let's go. I cannot accompany you into the chapel, but I will walk you there."

Rishe stood from her chair, weary. "Thank you..."

I mean, I knew he killed his mother before killing the emperor, so I thought I was past reeling at new rumors. Apparently not!

Oliver was coolly conversing with the priest at the door. Rishe sighed, quietly, so that he wouldn't notice. *I'm curious about Leo and Mistress Millia, but the biggest mysteries concern Prince Arnold.*

Holding back all the things she yearned to say, Rishe approached when Oliver waved her over. She followed the priest to the chapel on the eastern side of the Grand Basilica. Its thick door struck her as vaguely familiar.

Oliver stopped by the door, smiling. "This is as far as I can go. I'll see you later, Lady Rishe."

"Thank you, Oliver. Goodbye for now."

Rishe now had to enter the chapel and declare her engagement's annulment before the goddess's holy statue. Then the bishops would read some psalms, and the impurity of Rishe's annulled engagement would be cleansed from her body and soul once she fully absorbed the holy words. The process would take the rest of the day.

Other priests whispered about her as she passed by.

"Poor girl. She must listen to psalms for hours to annul an engagement ceremony, right? That is hard even for a devout believer."

"She'll be lucky if she's even allowed one break..."

Although Rishe could barely hear what they were saying, she had a pretty good idea from the movements of their lips. She gulped and steeled herself as she entered the chapel.

A few hours later...

Th-this is fun!

In the space totally reserved for her ceremony, Rishe trembled with excitement. The voices of the bishops echoed throughout the beautiful chapel. The psalms they read were translated from the original holy book. In her early days as a young noble lady, she'd heard these psalms countless times. Now, however, they had taken on new meaning for Rishe.

I can't believe the twelfth psalm is connected to the Qualuk Archipelago! She was on the edge of her seat listening to the bishops' voices. *I always thought the psalms were just artistic pieces crafted from pretty words, but that's not true at all. These are a grand tale of adventure starring the gods!*

She realized this soon after the first psalm began. Although she wouldn't have gleaned it from her noble education, her worldwide travels in other lives provided context for the psalms' imagery and more.

The "Breath of Frost" that the bishop just read must refer to the coasts of Qualuk in the winter. That means the Great Tides from the ninth psalm—meaning the ocean—should be showing up again soon, right? Yes, I knew it! The part where "even the flowers freeze" refers to how the ocean's surface resembles a field of white flowers when it ices over. It's so beautiful.

In her third life, she had investigated the phenomenon with Michel. Rishe's eyes sparkled with nostalgia as she remembered the sight of the frozen sea.

"And a great clap of thunder rang out, whereupon the lightning pierced the foaming earth, bringing a new dawn..."

I wonder if this will lead into a story about King Solnero. Princess Eusoness showed up earlier, so I assume he'll be next. I can't wait!

The bishop reading from the holy book glanced up at Rishe, wearing a look of consternation. After reading the twelfth psalm, he abruptly asked, "Why don't we take a break here? We've been going for quite a while."

"My, has it been that long already?" She ached to hear more, but it would have to wait. *As much as I wish he would go on, I'm sure the bishop is tired.*

She was honestly disappointed, and it showed plain on her face. Unsettled by this, the bishop hastened out of the chapel.

Rishe observed the light pouring into the room through the stained glass. *From the position of the sun, I'd say about three hours have passed.*

She stood, thinking back on her childhood memories. Out on the balcony, there was a mural with some psalms on it in their original language. She opened the balcony door and let the cool breeze caress her cheek. The balcony wall was bathed in the golden light of early evening. Rishe studied it, her eyes following the lines of carved text.

This is it—the goddess and the psalms. I haven't seen Crusade writing in a long time. Let's see, this line is..."The goddess gave unto the people her protection."

There were only excerpts from the psalms on the mural. Rishe relied heavily on her memories as she read through them. *"The royal priestess spread the goddess's unseen, unheard protection through the world. Guiding with love..."*

Rishe went back and forth reading them until she felt someone approaching. She glanced up in time to see a man step onto the balcony. He wore a bishop's robes embroidered with gold thread. Apparently, he was of a different rank than the bishops who read her the psalms.

"You must be Lady Rishe Irmgard Weitzner." The clergyman, who looked to be in his mid-thirties, gave her a friendly smile. He was tall and slim, and something about him seemed almost manufactured. "I am Kristoff Justus Traugott Schneider. I serve as the archbishop's aide."

"Bishop Schneider, I apologize for requesting this ceremony so suddenly."

"No need to apologize. It's lamentable that you could not wed the one you performed the engagement ceremony with, but that, too, is the goddess's will." Schneider scrutinized the mural Rishe had been reading from. "Written on this mural are portions of psalms concerning the goddess and the royal priestess. Isn't the writing strange? It's the Crusade language. The script and language are extremely difficult to learn, so there are only a handful of people who can read it."

"Crusade was the language the goddess spoke, wasn't it? That's why it's so different from our own language."

"Ah, so you're somewhat versed in the subject. It's exactly as you say. I'm embarrassed to say it took me a decade of studying to master it." He narrowed his eyes as if peering into the past. "The late royal priestess was highly proficient. I doubt we'll ever see someone of her fluency again."

"When you say 'late,' you mean...?"

"Yes, the royal priestess who died in an accident twenty-two years ago." Schneider's smile grew sad. "Did you know that the royal priestess is said to descend from the goddess? That's why only a woman born to the priestess's bloodline can be chosen for the position. Our previous priestess had a sister, but she was too frail for the role and passed away ten years ago."

"I see."

"There are a few men in the family, so the goddess's precious bloodline has not died out completely. Still, the fact remains that only a woman may play the role of the royal priestess."

As she listened, Rishe thought, *It's a very interesting topic, but why in the world is he telling me this?*

"I apologize. I intended to start with small talk, but I ended up rambling." Schneider surveyed the mural, his smile wry, before turning back to Rishe. He looked her gravely in the eye and said, "You must not marry Arnold Hein."

Rishe's breath caught at the unexpected words. "Now why—" she began, but she held her tongue when she noticed another man stepping out on the balcony.

Arnold leveled a glare at Schneider as cold as ice. The air crackled with tension, and the temperature seemed to drop by several degrees. "I believe I made myself clear when I said no one from the Church was to get anywhere near my wife outside of the ceremony."

Schneider hesitated but cleared his throat and managed, "I...I have to say I'm not impressed, Prince Arnold." He feigned composure, but it was clear that he was terrified of Arnold. Regardless, Schneider seemed intent on giving him his opinion. "Lady Rishe is not your wife but your fiancée. The goddess would not approve of you calling a woman you have not yet exchanged vows as your wife."

"Your point being?"

There was the sharp sound of a footstep. Schneider flinched. Arnold loped forward, pinning Schneider in place with his eyes.

"Erm, i-in the first place, the annulment rite is not yet finished."

"..."

"So, in the eyes of the goddess, you are not even Lady Rishe's fiancé. At this moment, she is still engaged to the crown prince of Hermity."

"I don't know if you can wrap your mind around the concept of differing values, but I will *never* get on my knees and beg forgiveness from the goddess." Arnold took Rishe's hand and pulled her toward him—or perhaps away from Schneider. He then turned his dark gaze on the bishop. "Not even if I committed the grievous sin of killing you."

Schneider paled and clenched his teeth. He left the balcony as if shot from it, totally unable to conjure a retort. As he hurried away, Rishe frowned, feeling awkward. *Um.*

She studied Arnold, who was still holding her hand. He glared at the door Schneider had disappeared into with the eyes of a territorial carnivore. *Someone's in a bad mood.*

Apparently, Arnold had warned the clergy not to approach Rishe. It was the first she heard of this, and she doubted he'd tell her the reason if asked. Instead, she broached another subject.

"Don't you think it's better not to call me your wife when we're only engaged?"

She knew full well this wasn't the first time he'd done it. Arnold sometimes referred to Rishe as his wife to third parties, despite her being his fiancée.

I'm sure there's a reason he does it. "Wife" was shorter than "fiancée," for instance. But they weren't married yet, and referring to her as such invited misunderstanding.

Arnold didn't seem the least bit remorseful. "It's a done deal, anyway."

"What is?"

"You becoming my wife."

He said it so matter-of-factly, Rishe felt her heart jump into her throat. She was worried she would yelp or do something just as embarrassing, so she covered her mouth with the hand Arnold hadn't grabbed.

The prince gave her a quizzical look. "What is it?"

"N-nothing..." Rishe mumbled, and Arnold looked even more dubious. Rishe removed her hand from her mouth and said quietly, "I don't think anything in life is a 'done deal,' Your Highness. You never know what will happen."

"Oh?"

"We may be engaged, but no one can predict the future, can they?" Dietrich was a perfect example. She'd performed the engagement ceremony with him, and Arnold knew how that had turned out. "And I don't just mean our engagement might not work out. For example...I could die before our wedding ceremony."

Arnold didn't respond.

I can't tell Prince Arnold I've died several times before, so it has to come off as hypothetical.

Rishe was about to cock her head and say, "Right?" but before she could, Arnold's free hand cupped her jaw.

Huh?

He gently but firmly turned her face up to his. With the light of the sunset behind him, Arnold studied her with narrowed eyes. "I won't allow that."

Rishe gulped. They were close enough to kiss, and it was rare for Arnold to be so commanding with her. *That's not very convincing, considering you're the reason for all my deaths so far, Your Highness!*

She couldn't voice the objection aloud. No point in saying it to the current Prince Arnold, anyway.

Having no possible way of knowing her thoughts, Arnold's face inched even closer to hers, eyes never leaving her face. "What's your answer?"

His voice was husky and just a little sweet. Rishe felt like she was being scolded and comforted at the same time. She was speechless as she peered into Arnold's crystalline blue eyes.

"Tell me you understand, or I'll make you understand like I did before."

"Eep!"

Arnold ran his thumb across the corner of her lips. He didn't quite touch them, but it was a clear warning. She squeaked, her back tickled by the shiver running down her spine.

When he said "before," he meant the time when he'd suddenly

kissed her. His hands were gentle, but there was a hardness to his gaze. Rishe managed to squeeze out a response. "You're teasing me again..."

His last kiss *had* been rather forceful. She didn't know his motives, but she knew that Arnold tended to act like a villain when he wanted to hide something.

"I-I can tell that much. You're not the type to be cruel for no reason, Prince Arnold."

"I wonder about that."

"Huh?" The moment Rishe's eyes went wide, Arnold drew her closer. He looked down at Rishe with his intense eyes. Because he was still holding her chin, she couldn't look away from him. He bent over her right then and there.

Remembering their last kiss, Rishe squeezed her eyes shut. At the same time, she could feel his lips stop just before her own.

Their lips were so close, but they weren't touching. Rishe could feel his body heat through the air between them. If either Rishe or Arnold made the slightest move, they would be having their second kiss.

"Nnngh..." Rishe's eyes were shut so tight, her eyelashes quivered. She sensed Arnold blink, so she knew his eyes weren't closed. She was sure he was watching her until he slowly pulled away.

"Phew!" Rishe let out the breath she was holding. She didn't even know when she'd stopped breathing.

I-I really thought he was going to kiss me...

He surely wouldn't have, but it was bad for her heart all the same. Rishe held her burning cheeks with both hands, taking deep breaths to calm down.

Arnold just sighed and frowned. "Anyway, I'm not going to follow orders from the Church. I have no reason to listen to them. Just remember that."

"A-all right..." she said, a hand over her chest where her heart was still thrumming.

Heaving another sigh, Arnold asked, "What did that bishop want with you?"

He warned me not to marry you. Rishe kept quiet about that and glanced at the mural. "I was reading the psalms here, and he came out to explain them to me."

She didn't tell him the full truth, but she also didn't lie.

Arnold looked at her curiously. "You can read this?"

"I studied the language for a time, but I had to stop. There are a lot of parts I'm unsure about."

"Like what?" Arnold asked, and Rishe blinked.

He waited for her answer, so she pointed out an area of the mural. "That section there. Normally, you'd read the second word as 'spring,' but I feel like there are other readings as well."

Arnold looked up at the mural and said offhandedly, "You read it as 'flower.'"

Rishe gaped at him.

Arnold observed the mural with disinterest and, as if reading their own language, gave a smooth explanation, "That word is most often interpreted as 'open.' Next is the 'spring' meaning you mentioned. There's a less popular third meaning, which is 'flower,' something that opens in spring."

"Th-then, if it's referring to a flower instead of spring, does that change the way you read the words before and after it too?"

"It does. That whole line would be read as 'the girl with hair the color of flowers.'"

"Wow..." It was just as Arnold said. His interpretation of the line matched the rest of the text. She was impressed by his abilities, but she could also hardly believe what she was hearing. "Your Highness, can you read Crusade?"

"What's written here, at least."

"Are you—these are *original* psalms! Their interpretation is so difficult that there is a whole field of study devoted to it!"

This was a language the archbishop's aide had spent an entire decade learning. Rishe could only read a little of it because she'd had an opportunity to study the language once upon a time. She hadn't even come close to mastering it, so how had Arnold picked up as much as he had?

"Wh-what about that phrase there? If you translate it directly, it comes out to 'the seasons pass with the girl's guidance,' but that just doesn't feel right to me."

"It's closer to 'the seasons repeat with the girl's guidance.' It likely refers to the festival at which the royal priestess performs."

"How can you tell?"

"It says she 'sings' here," he said simply.

Rishe was flabbergasted. *He's beautiful and excellent with a sword, gifted at both politics and strategy,* and *he's classically educated? Isn't this guy a little too perfect?!*

The Crusade language was specialist knowledge; it certainly wasn't something everyone learned. Even Church bishops normally used sacred texts translated into their mother tongues.

Come to think of it, there was that rumor that the current emperor of Galkhein is a devout believer, and that's the reason he didn't invade Domana, home of the Grand Basilica. If that rumor is true, and he gave Prince Arnold a special education for that reason... maybe that's why His Highness hates the Crusade so much.

As Rishe puzzled this, a cold wind blew past them. The gust lifted Rishe's hair, and she reflexively held it down with one hand. When she realized what she was doing, she peered at her own hair and gasped.

"Prince Arnold."

"What?"

"I'm not part of the royal priestess's bloodline."

Arnold frowned. "What's that supposed to mean?"

"That line you told me earlier, about the girl with hair the color of flowers. It goes on to say that the girl with hair the color of flowers was descended from the goddess and led the people as the royal priestess, right?"

"It does."

"That would mean women who are qualified to be the royal priestess have hair the color of flowers, but..." Rishe looked down at her wavy hair. It was a yellow-tinged pink. Coral would be the closest comparison, but she could see it being compared to a flower as well. "I get my hair color from my redheaded mother and blond father. It's a rare color, but there's no particular meaning to it."

"..."

"The most significant aspect of my lineage is my father descending from the royal family of Hermity. I don't believe I have any blood from the goddess." Rishe pouted, somehow feeling sorrier the longer she went on.

"What are you talking about?" Arnold asked with a scowl.

"Well, I was wondering if you proposed to me because you thought I was the last remaining candidate to become the royal priestess."

Bishop Schneider had just told her that all the women qualified to become the royal priestess had passed away.

"If there were still a woman with the royal priestess's blood hidden somewhere, marrying her would provide Galkhein with significant power, wouldn't it?"

"..."

"But I have nothing to do with the royal priestess. If I gave you the wrong impression and you proposed to me for that reason, then I'm sorry..."

"..."

"Wh-what are you making that face for?"

Arnold regarded Rishe like he was exasperated from the bottom of his heart. While Rishe contemplated how to reply, unsure as to what had brought this reaction on, he sighed for the umpteenth time that day and said, "Do you remember how Kyle compared you to the goddess the other day?"

Rishe remembered the conversation. In this life, the first time she met Kyle, he'd told her, *"Your beauty is like that of a goddess."* He was just performing the peculiar social niceties of Coyolles, so Rishe hadn't really been listening. But now that she thought about it, perhaps it explained why Arnold had been so annoyed back then.

Ah! I wonder if the reason Prince Arnold made such a scary face was because the word "goddess" came up? She'd always wondered why he'd glared so hard at Kyle, but it finally started to make sense. She was beginning to see exactly how much he hated the Church too. Rishe nodded to herself, having come to her own conclusions, and Arnold looked at her in silence.

"Even if the goddess herself manifested before me, I'd have no interest in her, let alone her bloodline."

Rishe blinked. With that serious look in his eyes, Arnold looked even more handsome than usual.

His gaze still firmly fixed on her, he said, "There's only one person I'll ever kneel to."

In Galkhein, men kneeled and kissed the back of a woman's hand to propose. Remembering the occasion, Rishe felt her cheeks flush. Arnold smirked when he saw how flustered she'd become. He reached out with one of his big hands and ruffled her hair.

"I'm in a much better mood now. I'll go get back to work."

H-he's just teasing me! She wanted to protest, but she was struggling to form words. All she was able to squeak out was a weak "See you later." It was mortifying.

After watching Arnold leave, Rishe sighed. She took several steadying breaths, waiting for her cheeks to cool.

Eventually, a monk stepped onto the balcony. "I'm terribly sorry, Lady Rishe. The ceremony was paused for a routine break, but it seems it will take a little longer for it to resume," the monk said.

Rishe cocked her head. "That's fine. Did something happen?"

"W-well..." The monk frowned, as if deeply perplexed, and said, "It seems our stand-in royal priestess has confined herself to her room."

***

Once Rishe left the chapel, she strolled the courtyard alone.

"It seems Lady Millia disliked the festival costume we prepared for her," the monk had said, his shoulders slumped. *"The duke and all the bishops acquainted with Lady Millia are stationed by her door, trying to persuade her. Any final adjustments to the costume need to be made by tomorrow morning or we won't make it in time for the festival."*

It seemed there was now quite a commotion outside her room. The bishop performing Rishe's ceremony must've scurried off to aid the persuasion effort.

In response to the news, Rishe had suggested delaying her ceremony and asked for the location of Millia's room. Rather than head to the hall where the duke and bishops were gathered, however, she'd made for the courtyard behind the building with the guest rooms. She came with a certain purpose in mind but discovered something unexpected along the way.

There's just one little footprint here. The footprint was oriented toward the forest surrounding the Grand Basilica. Whoever left it had headed there. *When we arrived, we were told that the forest was sacred ground and therefore not to be disturbed.*

Examining the footprint, she determined that it belonged to a boy's shoe. Leaving it aside for now, she gazed up at the guest rooms. At that exact moment, she heard a familiar shrill voice coming from the easternmost window on the third floor.

"I am *only* wearing a pink dress to the festival!"

A flock of birds resting in the courtyard trees were spooked into flight. Next, Rishe heard the duke's voice.

"Millia! How many times do I have to tell you to be reasonable?!"

Well, the two of them seem to be in good health, at least. I'm glad. Rishe was relieved to hear their voices, even if they were quarreling. Although they may not have been badly hurt, a carriage crash was a terrifying experience. She'd been concerned about their mental and emotional state, but the vigor in their shouts assuaged her worries.

The window and curtains of the room had been left open. From where Rishe was standing, she could see Millia's back.

It does sound like there are a few people on the other side of the door as well. That's only going to make Mistress Millia dig her heels in!

Rishe scanned her surroundings to make sure she was alone, then peered up at a tree adjacent to Millia's room. She hiked up her skirts, revealing a dagger strapped to her thigh. She left the dagger and removed the belt holding it in place. A makeshift grappling hook was tied to it.

Now then...

Millia's voice was still coming from the window above her. "Why won't you understand?! It was my strange power that did that to the carriage!"

"Don't be silly. That was an accident! The carriage's wheel broke down!"

"No! It's because of my power! If you don't listen to me, something bad's going to happen again!"

"Oh, come now, Millia!"

"Everyone get away from the door! If you don't, it'll—" Millia's voice broke off. She swiveled toward the window and froze. "Huh? Whaaat?!"

Hopping down from the window into the room, Rishe smiled at the duke's daughter. "Hello, Lady Millia." She patted her skirts down and wound up the grappling hook. When she combed her fingers through her tresses, she smoothly picked off a leaf.

"Millia? Millia, what's wrong?" the duke called out from the other side of the door.

"N-nothing!" Millia chirped. She whirled on Rishe and asked, in hushed alarm, "H-how did you get in here? This is the third floor, and you came in through the window!"

Rishe brought a finger to her lips and grinned mischievously. "It's a secret. You'll keep it a secret from everyone else that I was here too, won't you?"

Millia's eyes widened, then her expression turned solemn. "You have a strange power just like I do."

Not really, but I wouldn't want Mistress Millia to imitate me. Rishe kept that thought to herself and knelt in front of Millia. "Lady Millia, what exactly do you dislike about your festival dress? It's that white one over there, isn't it? It's so cute!"

The girl looked down at the floor and murmured, "My mama is dead." Millia's tiny fingers fiddled with her soft violet locks. "She always said I was her little princess, so pink princess dresses looked good on me. If I'm going to be the royal priestess's stand-in, I want to wear a pink dress like Mama said I should."

Rishe likewise lowered her eyes. *Mistress Millia is lying.* Millia had a habit of playing with her hair when she fibbed. That said, it was true that Millia's mother had often dressed her in pink. *I do think she wants to wear pink, but she's lying about the reason. Why lie about that, though?*

"Well, Lady Millia, would you like me to turn this dress pink for you?"

"What?!" Millia's honey-colored eyes bulged at the unexpected suggestion. "W-with magic? With magic, right?"

"No, not magic. I can use dyes to make it whatever color you want, though."

"Dyes, you say..."

"It looks to be fabric that won't shrink if it gets wet. Once the final adjustments are completed, you can make any additional embellishments yourself, yes? Turning a white dress pink, for instance, and maybe adding some flower ornaments to it."

The way Millia's eyes sparkled at the idea was just too cute.

Rishe smiled warmly, explaining, "They're very fun to make, but they take time. I don't think we'll be able to get them done in time for the festival if they don't finish the adjustments today."

"I-I'll do it right now!" Millia slapped a hand over her mouth after she realized what she'd blurted out. "Oops..."

With a chuckle, Rishe stood up. "Please open the door for your father, then...but first, could you close your eyes for a minute?"

She waited for Millia to obey before going to the window for her descent. It was much easier and faster to get down than it was to climb up. Once her feet touched the earth, she called, "You can open your eyes now!"

Millia gaped at her from the window. "N-no way!"

Rishe put a finger to her lips once more and, after watching her former mistress nod in response, bowed politely and returned the way she'd come.

I'll need to investigate Mistress Millia and Prince Arnold, but there's one other person I should look into in this life. Rishe checked for any passersby and headed toward the forest. *The forest was said to be sacred ground when I came here in my last life, but I don't remember it being off-limits.*

The faint footprint she'd seen earlier had been left by a child. The markings appeared to be from a masculine shoe, so it wasn't Millia's. It also looked like it had been left in the last few hours or so.

Maybe one footprint is nothing to worry over, but if a person of interest is going into a forbidden forest, then I can't just leave it be, can I?

Rishe ventured through the woodland outskirts, erasing her own footprints before she got too close. She made her way inside, silent and stealthy. Soon enough, she heard quiet footsteps approaching.

"Hello, Leo."

"Ack!" Leo yelped when she addressed him, his innocent eyes bugging out at her. "You were with the crown prince of Galkhein."

It's the second time today someone was surprised by my calling out to them, Rishe thought as she smiled at Leo.

Leo was giving her a cautious look. "The forest is off-limits past here."

"I know. And I know you've been in there."

"You're mistaken. I was just looking for some flowers I could use to decorate my master's room. I was going to turn back after coming this far." Leo was unusually blunt for his age, but he seemed softer than he'd been compared to the scarred version of him in her life as a knight.

Rishe surveyed him. "See how there's a piece of zaott moss sticking to your pants?"

Leo gasped.

"That moss only grows where there isn't much sunlight. In a dense forest, for instance."

The boy scowled and looked away. "Are you gonna lecture me? Or are you gonna hand me over to the Church?"

"I won't do either, but I *do* want you to take me somewhere."

"Where?"

"Well, naturally..." Rishe grinned and pointed behind him. "Into the forbidden forest."

"Wha...?" Leo retreated a step, thoroughly appalled. "Aren't you supposed to be an adult? What're you up to?" He was like a feral cat unused to humans, fit to start hissing at any moment. "Can Galkhein's crown princess break the Church's taboos?"

"Well, the only person who will know I've been out here is the one who was out here with me."

"Urgh..."

"I'm a bad lady, so if someone points out that I've got moss on me, I'll just play dumb," she said, smiling wider.

Leo clicked his tongue in frustration. "If I take you, will you stay quiet about me being here?"

"I'll stay quiet even if you don't, so no need to worry."

At that, the boy blinked his wide eyes in bewilderment.

"I'd be happy if you did take me, though," Rishe added. "The sun is about to set, so I must return soon or my betrothed will be angry with me."

Leo frowned, turned around, and walked off into the forest. Rishe thanked him and followed.

If this were the Leo from my life as a knight, he wouldn't have taken me.

In all likelihood, he wouldn't have spoken to her either. He would have just ignored her, and it would have ended right there. Even after he'd started talking to her a little bit, he probably would have just said, "Why should I have to do that? Go away," or "Don't involve me in the first platoon's antics."

It's been a long time since I was last in a forest. I'll have to make sure I'm taking regularly spaced steps and counting them. By doing that, she could get a vague idea of the distance she'd traveled. It was important to have a sense of where you were when traveling through a place with scant visual landmarks, like a forest or a mountain.

Leo and Rishe walked at about the same pace. Counting her paces on her hands, Rishe spoke to him from behind. "I heard your name from Duke Jonal earlier. I'm Rishe. It's nice to meet you."

"..."

"I wound up with some free time, so I wanted to explore the area around the Grand Basilica. Lucky that you passed by when you did!"

"..."

"What *were* you doing out here in the first place?"

"I heard Mistress Millia was throwing a fit," Leo said at length. "I was slacking off someplace where no one would look for me. I didn't want to get dragged into something annoying."

The Leo in my sixth loop said the same thing all the time. Deep down, he really was the same Leo she knew.

Smiling to herself, Rishe brought up something else that piqued her curiosity. "I'm surprised you got permission to enter the Grand Basilica, Leo. They're barely letting anyone in because it's almost time for the festival, right?"

"It's just Master looking out for me."

"What do you mean by that?"

"I grew up in an orphanage near here."

This was news to her. *Duke Jonal took Leo along so he could come visit his childhood home?*

She'd heard that it was quite an involved process to bring a servant into the Grand Basilica around this time. Normally, the royal priestess would be staying there, and they'd have to vet each visiting person extensively. That was why Rishe had left her maids behind in Galkhein and Arnold had only brought along Oliver. As for the knights who had accompanied them on their journey here, they were staying in a nearby town.

I'm curious about a few things, but...

Rishe glanced around the area. The red-tinged dusk was shining into the forest. All the brush and shrubbery made it easy for her to pick out animal trails. A tree a short distance away bore some sort of marking. She peered at the signs of disturbed grass and fur clinging to the trees and pondered.

"From here on, please step exactly where I'm stepping," Leo told her.

"Oh? Why?"

"There could be venomous snakes in the grass. If you get bitten by a snake, it'll be a big to-do and they'll find out I was here."

"Appreciated, but it's all right." Rishe stopped and smiled. "I'll be fine on my own now."

"What?" Leo spun around, eyes round, like he was staring at some unknown creature.

"Thank you for taking me this far, but I can handle it from here. You should head back to the Basilica," Rishe said, tucking her hair behind her ear. She could sense Leo's wariness mounting.

"Seriously, what are you thinking?"

"Nothing you need to be so concerned about. I just don't want to trouble you any more than I already have."

"I'm staying too."

She blinked, surprised.

"The sun will fully set soon, and it's dangerous to be in the forest all by yourself. If something happened to you, they'd suspect me and I'd be punished."

Rishe found herself remembering the Leo with the eyepatch. "Your master doesn't seem like the type of person who'd let that happen."

"Whatever. I said I'm staying. If there's something you want to do in this forest, hurry up and do it."

"Are you sure? I'll take you up on your offer, then."

"Ah!" Leo cried out when Rishe took a step forward. He was shocked because Rishe had slipped out of the path of his footsteps and ventured deeper into the forest on her own. "Wait! I told you if you don't watch where you're going, you might get bitten by a venomous snake!"

"The snakes that live on this continent may be venomous, but they're also cowardly. They'll flee if they see a human, and they won't emerge from their dens if they hear people talking in the first place."

"Even if that's true, it could still happen!"

"Actually, there's something far more dangerous out here than snakes."

Rishe stopped in front of a thick tree with a mark on its trunk. Leo gave chase and stopped right behind her. She picked up a fallen branch and dug through the grass around the marked tree. Eventually, she found exactly what she expected.

"I knew it."

Hidden under the fallen leaves and weeds was a bear trap—two semicircular jaws with sharp serrated edges. It was designed to snap shut on the leg of whatever unsuspecting creature was unfortunate enough to trigger it.

"How did you know there was a trap there?"

"Because of the mark on the tree. You put a mark only a human would recognize on the tree so that you don't lose track of your trap."

Crouching down, Rishe inspected the device. The trap's vicious metal teeth shone with iridescent light. She took out a handkerchief and wiped the surface of the trap, careful not to trigger it. Then she brought the handkerchief to her nose.

Wet...and smells metallic.

Rishe stood and approached another tree, broken branch in hand. She didn't need to investigate to know what sort of trap was laid here. She reached out as far as she could and pressed the branch to the ground. There was a *whump*, and the ground vanished.

"A pit trap?!"

"This is dangerous, so stay back, Leo," Rishe said, getting out her grappling hook. She threw one end of the rope straight up, catching the hook on a tree branch. She tugged hard on it to make sure it was secure, then peered into the pit while holding on to the rope.

It's about a meter across...and a meter deep, looks like. Spikes set at the bottom. The metal stakes were poking out between the fallen leaves in the pit. Gripping the rope for support, Rishe reached down into the pit and wiped one of the stakes with her handkerchief. *This trap is the same. The metallic smell is strong, but this chemical smells just as much. I've had a few run-ins with this scent.*

She voiced her conviction aloud: "They're coated in poison."

Leo grimaced. "To finish off their prey? But this is a forbidden forest, so why are there hunter's traps here?"

"Someone is using the fact that the forest is off-limits to their advantage."

"Um, why are you wiping all those spikes with your handkerchief?"

"I want to find out what poison the hunters around here use. I need to take samples when I can or it'll be a real pain trying to get one later." He frowned even harder, so she tilted her head in puzzlement. "What's wrong?"

His reply emerged slow and deliberate. "I've heard some nobles and royals employ lookalikes to keep them safe from assassins."

"It's not very well known, but yes, some countries do that. Why do you mention it?"

"You're not a good body double."

"Huh?"

Leo studied Rishe and declared, "You should find another job. You act way too weird. No one would believe you're the crown princess!"

She spent several moments racking her brain for a response to Leo's genuine concern, but in the end, she had nothing to give.

***

Rishe had no choice but to let Leo think she was the crown princess's body double. His eyes had been so full of confidence, she'd been absolutely sure she could never convince him otherwise.

After returning to the Basilica, Rishe found herself alone in the dining hall. She sighed, thinking back to the exchange she'd had with Leo.

"Er...I'm not a body double."

In contrast to Rishe's hesitancy, Leo was firm and earnest. *"All body doubles say that. At least, I'm guessing they do."*

"I'm sure they do! Anyway, I could see the need for a body double for the crown prince, but why his fiancée or wife?"

"Look, it's okay. You said you wouldn't tell anyone that I went into the forest, right?" Leo looked her right in the eye. *"I promise you the same thing: I won't tell anyone you're a fake."*

Once again, Rishe had been stunned into silence. All she could do in response to his strange, trustworthy promise was thank him vaguely.

Well, I suppose there's no real reason I need to correct him...but Leo is oddly caring despite how blunt he is, Rishe thought as she moved her knife and fork.

The dining hall was far too big for her to use all by herself, but there was still no sign of Arnold. His business must have been delayed by the commotion Millia caused before sundown.

After Rishe finished her meal and capped it off with tea, Oliver arrived. "I'm sorry my lord couldn't join you for dinner," he said. "Lady Rishe, His Grace and the Church have a request of you."

"Regarding Lady Millia, I presume?"

"Yes. It seems like you have some idea already, but they would like your assistance in preparing for the festival." Still standing in the entryway, Oliver put a hand to his heart and said, "Lady Millia herself is quite insistent upon your presence."

M-my darling Mistress! Rishe felt a twinge in her heart. She wanted to accept right away, but she knew she wasn't in a position to make the decision on her own.

"Does Prince Arnold know about this?"

"No, I thought I should ascertain your feelings on the matter first."

"Because you need to find a way to ask him without ruining his mood first?"

"Ha ha ha." A bright smile appeared on Oliver's face, but he didn't endeavor to hide the truth in the slightest.

Rishe pressed a hand to her forehead and set the teacup back on its saucer. *I don't know why, but Prince Arnold didn't want the Church interacting with me. I have no idea how he'd react to their asking me to help prepare for the festival.* At the very least, she couldn't imagine the conversation being very amicable.

She thought for some time, then said, "Oliver, I'd like to tell His Highness about this myself."

"I cannot let you trouble yourself, Lady Rishe."

"But—"

"I will accept my lord's wrath. If anything, I'd appreciate your help with the recovery afterward, Lady Rishe."

"The *recovery*, Oliver?" With such frightening repercussions, surely it made more sense for her to negotiate with Arnold.

If I can spend some more time with Mistress Millia, that'd be incredibly convenient. Further contact will enable me to look deeper into the mistress's "curse," Duke Jonal's change of heart, and Leo's injuries. Plus, helping out with the festival might give me more of a glimpse into why Arnold detests the Church so much. Still, Oliver shouldn't have to get in trouble because I'm doing whatever I want.

Oliver smiled wryly while she was lost in thought. "You're too kind, Lady Rishe. I'm sure that's why Lady Millia trusts you so much. If she'd clung to my lord instead of you on first meeting, the situation would have doubtless taken a turn for the worse."

"There's nothing special about me, but I certainly can't imagine how the two of them might interact. Besides, His Highness told me he doesn't like children."

The attendant looked astounded. "He should never have said such a thing to his future wife."

"Huh?" Rishe's eyes widened in surprise.

Oliver bowed his head solemnly. "I sincerely apologize, Lady Rishe. I will be sure to have some strict words with my lord later on. I can't believe him! It's like he doesn't even understand that one day he'll have to raise an heir."

"Um, no, it's totally fine! Please don't worry about it! I just, erm..." Rishe hurriedly changed the subject. "Children? Right, childhood! What was Prince Arnold like as a child?!"

"My lord?"

"Yes! I would love to hear about it!" It was a spur-of-the-moment question, but she *was* interested.

Although Oliver was a little taken aback, he obliged. "He was an incredibly brilliant crown prince. I first met him ten years ago, but I'd heard of his reputation before then. Rumors of his genius were not confined to Galkhein alone. For instance, when the previous ruler of Halil Rasha—the desert country—came to visit, he would always bring his son and have the boys exchange ideas and spar together."

"His son" must be King Zahad. Now that she thought about it, King Zahad seemed to have met Arnold several times in the past. In Rishe's first loop, it was Zahad who had informed her that Arnold started the war. She found herself remembering Zahad's aggressive expression at the time. *Prince Arnold and King Zahad may be alike in age, but they're both royals of countries with a similar level of power. Moreover, the way they think is completely different. I seriously doubt they'd get along.*

The desert country of Halil Rasha was one of the few nations that could put up a fight against Galkhein when Arnold went to war in the future. Rishe began to feel faint, imagining the sparks that would fly when Arnold and Zahad met at their wedding. She shook off the feeling, however, since there was no point stressing about that now.

"When you met the nine-year-old Prince Arnold, was he exactly like the rumors said, Oliver?"

"Well, I was summoned to the imperial palace and I knelt in an audience room, waiting for him to appear. When my lord sat in the seat before me and I was given permission to raise my head, I was shocked," Oliver said with a somewhat strained smile. "The first time I saw my lord, he was covered in wounds from head to toe."

Rishe's eyes widened.

"There was a big piece of gauze on his tiny cheek, bandages wrapped around his head, and a bunch of little wounds on his arms and fingers. Bright-red blood was seeping through the bandages around his neck, like the wound there just wouldn't close. It looked like the sort of laceration that would make an adult moan in anguish from the pain and heat."

There was an old scar on Arnold's neck. It was a large, deep wound—like he had been stabbed multiple times with a knife.

"But my young lord was just sitting in the chair, completely composed. His face betrayed not an ounce of anguish. In fact, he had his chin in his hand, and his eyes were like ice."

She hadn't been there to witness it, but Rishe could picture it vividly in her mind's eye. Nine was younger than the current Leo and Millia. Yet at that age, Arnold had already been wearing his trademark deadpan expression, even with a terrible injury. Rishe could imagine the peculiar sight perfectly.

"He was already quite handsome back then, which only contributed to his intimidating presence. My lord wielded an incredible sense of gravity for a child of his age. All the servants nearby were trembling in awe of him."

"Earlier today, you told me he killed all of his servants."

"Yes, and that's why he still has so few."

Rishe held her tongue after Oliver's nonchalant statement. She understood that he said the words lightly because he didn't intend to elaborate.

"A lot of things happened back then, and I chose to serve my lord. After he recovered from his injuries, he began to display even more of his talents, you see... However, regardless of his growth as a crown prince, he remained a somewhat twisted human being." Oliver regarded Rishe like an older brother talking about his younger sibling. "That's why I'm so relieved that he chose someone like you to be his wife, Lady Rishe."

Rishe blinked, not expecting the turn in conversation. "I haven't done anything to help His Highness."

"That isn't true. And my lord truly seems to enjoy himself when he's with you. I've never heard him call someone else's name so gently before."

"Ugh..." Now she was going to feel embarrassed whenever Arnold so much as said her name. Rishe hung her head, and Oliver blinked with the same surprise she'd just shown.

"Lately, you seem to have changed yourself, Lady Rishe."

"Huh?!"

"When you first arrived in Galkhein, I told you I had never seen my lord so happy before, but you didn't seem as pleased to hear it back then. I'm delighted to see that the two of you are cozying up." He chuckled good-naturedly at that.

"N-no! I didn't mean anything by it!"

What *had* she meant, then? *I* am *happy when His Highness smiles now.* That was true, and there was nothing she could do about it.

Rishe leapt to her feet and curtsied to Oliver. "I'm going to call for Prince Arnold. He may still have work to do, but he needs to eat!"

"A splendid idea. I think if you say something to him, my lord will hurry to finish his work."

"P-pardon me, then!" She straightened up and rushed out of the dining hall, heading east of the Basilica without so much as a backward glance.

"My lord is so cruel to his future wife," Oliver muttered after she left.

***

Augh, my cheeks are burning now because of all those strange thoughts!

As Rishe approached the building Arnold was in, the night air cooled her face and brought her back to earth. She let her intuition guide her, entering a hall and searching for the room where Arnold would be meeting with the bishops.

That instant, she heard a voice.

"It seems like Lady Rishe will make a wonderful empress for you."

Huh?!

It was Bishop Schneider, the archbishop's aide.

Not another weird conversation! Oh, I sense Prince Arnold too. Rishe screeched to a halt just in time to hear Arnold's voice coming from around a bend ahead.

"I don't believe the Church has any business evaluating my wife."

It seemed like it was just Arnold and Schneider. Rishe minimized her presence and heard Schneider speak candidly.

"Your Highness, all marriages are united with the blessing of the goddess and the Church. We are involved in your marriage whether you like it or not."

"Drop it. Besides, the question of what sort of empress she'll be is meaningless." Arnold's voice was even colder and more brusque than usual. "She's just a trophy wife."

Rishe gulped, hidden around the corner from the conversation.

"Wh-what are you saying? You looked like a loving couple earlier."

"She'll be a convenient tool for me. I'm just treating her as decently as I need to before we tie the knot. Once we're officially wed, I will have nothing to do with her anymore. I'll lock her up in the detached palace and let her rot." His tone was one of annoyance, but his words carried real weight.

Schneider sounded unsettled. "'Rot away'...?! Treating your wife in such a way goes against the goddess's will!"

"I don't give a damn."

"Your Highness!"

Rishe pondered for a moment, then retreated without making a sound. She counted ten long seconds and rounded the corner, announcing her presence with her footsteps.

Bishop Schneider glanced at her nervously. "My, if it isn't Lady Rishe."

She smiled at him and said, "Good evening." Then she looked up at Arnold and beamed, wrapping herself around his arm. "I missed you, Prince Arnold!"

He flinched beneath her embrace, but he didn't let his surprise show on his face. As he regarded her with his usual stoic expression, she pouted like a child. "Is *this* where you've been? You were so late coming back that I had to have dinner alone, you know."

"..."

"I wish you went to see me after finishing your work, like you *always* do. I hope you haven't forgotten that I want to be with you as much as possible." Still clinging to Arnold's arm, Rishe rested her head against it. She pretended to be angry, looking up at him covetously...as if she hadn't heard a bit of their conversation.

Now, how will His Highness respond? They were in front of the bishop, but Rishe tightened her grip on the prince. Arnold furrowed his brow, but it was only for a second. *As long as my little act hasn't gone overboard, we should be good.*

"I'm sorry," Arnold said at length. It was just as she suspected. Arnold's eyes were downcast as he gave her a mollifying pat on the head. "I finally finished my work just now. I was trying to hurry, but it seems I made you lonely."

The most beautiful fingers in the world combed through her coral-colored hair. He gently tucked a lock behind her ear. Then he looked right into her eyes and said, "I was on my way to dinner. Will you join me?"

"Of course, Prince Arnold. If you don't mind, would you tell me about your day while you eat?" Rishe smiled as if this were a regular exchange between them. To the bishop, she said, "Please forgive my selfishness, Bishop, but may I have His Highness for the rest of the night?" She rubbed her cheek against Arnold's arm to make a show of her claim.

Schneider, who was speechless at this exchange, cleared his throat and nodded. "Of course. The goddess values labor, but not at the cost of one's health. If you'll excuse me, I must be going as well." With that, Schneider scuttled off.

As she watched him go, Rishe thought about their earlier exchange. *"You must not marry Arnold Hein."* So the bishop had warned her. She had to find out why soon. That was another reason to help with Millia's participation in the festival. As she mulled it over, Arnold spoke a single word.

"Rishe."

"Yes?"

His voice was coming from awfully close.

"Eep..."

The moment Rishe realized why, her face went pale. She was *still* clinging to Arnold's arm.

"Ack!"

With a yelp, she detached herself. She raised both hands and apologized, doing her best to assert her lack of ill will. "I-I'm sorry! I was thinking, and I forgot I was still holding your arm! Also, I'm sorry for clinging to you without asking!"

"Why are you apologizing?" Arnold scrunched his brow and gave her a meaningful look. "You were listening, right? When I called you a trophy wife."

"Well, of course I was." Rishe cocked her head and looked back at him. "You didn't expect me to take you at your word, did you?" Her question was sincere, but Arnold seemed surprised. "I thought maybe you were saying it to support my plan to live a lazy life as crown princess, but...there's no reason for you to tell the Church about that."

"..."

"So, I just decided to go along with what you were saying. I don't know your true intentions, but you wanted to convince the bishop, right? I thought I'd play the part of a bad wife who doesn't doubt your love for her one bit," she explained, and the crease in his brow deepened more and more.

She didn't know why he looked so displeased, but there was one thing she *did* know. *Prince Arnold must have noticed me standing there.* Even though she was out of his line of sight around the corner, she was sure he had sensed her loitering there and heard her footsteps. He only said what he'd said because he had a reason to. That was why she'd turned back and announced her presence so blatantly, playing the ignorant fiancée.

Arnold grimaced for a while before finally saying, "I don't think you were exactly acting like a 'bad wife' back there."

"What? Did I mess up?!"

"That's not what I meant." He looked down and sighed. "I was prepared for you to slap me."

"Huh?" Rishe hadn't expected to hear that. *Does he feel guilty about what he said?* If Rishe had just walked out in the middle of their conversation, then there wouldn't have been any point in lying to Schneider. "It would be more satisfying for me to know your motives than to slap you, Your Highness."

He didn't respond.

"Don't worry. I don't expect you to tell me. Anyway, let's get you some dinner."

The monks were preparing their meals for the duration of their stay at the Grand Basilica. Since Rishe had been drinking tea just a minute ago, their cooking fires were likely still lit. *Should I have Oliver send for dinner?*

Arnold derailed her train of thought. "You shouldn't trust people who don't tell you anything."

Rishe whirled around and blinked at him, lashes fluttering. There was a dark light in Arnold's sea-colored eyes. It must have been the lighting in the hallway.

"If you do, you'll end up being a convenient tool for me."

"Your Highness." Rishe held his gaze, not letting go. "Trusting people is about more than just words."

"What?"

Maybe Arnold hadn't realized that his behavior thus far had been more than worthy of her trust.

"I told you on the balcony earlier, didn't I? That you're not the type to be cruel for no reason." Rishe paused to smile at him before continuing, "I won't tell you to trust me too, but you should understand that I'm not one to be discouraged by someone keeping me at a distance."

Arnold's eyes wavered. He sighed and then dropped his gaze. "I'm beginning to catch on."

If that was true, Rishe was glad for it.

He raised his head and told her, "Let me apologize for what I said. What would you like me to do?"

"You don't need to apologize. I don't intend to merely be a convenient fiancée for you, so don't worry about that!" She grinned at him, and Arnold went wary.

Heh heh heh, looks like he's a little nervous. I fully plan on taking advantage of his guilt!

Negotiations were most advantageous when the other party was feeling remorseful. This lesson from Rishe's life as a merchant was still proving useful.

"First of all, I would like to help Lady Millia with her preparations for the festival, so please permit me to do so."

"Preparations for the festival?" Arnold asked sourly. "The Church asked you to do that?"

"What do the details matter? If you'll permit me to ask for one more thing..."

"..."

"On second thought, let me add two things. And if I think of anything else, we can add them to the negotiating table!"

In the end, Rishe got Arnold to agree to every one of her requests.

CHAPTER 3

On their second day at the Grand Basilica, Rishe and Arnold had breakfast in the dining hall, after which she saw him off to his duties and returned to her room. She took out a leather trunk filled with small bottles from under her bed.

After some contemplation on the contents, she retrieved three of the bottles. The uneven dents in the sparkling glass gave them a flowerlike shape. She stuffed the bottles in a small bag and headed for the floor Millia's room was on.

Duke Jonal stood in front of the door.

"Good morning, Your Grace."

"If it isn't Lady Rishe." The duke turned to Rishe and put a hand to his chest, bowing politely. "I'm sorry. My daughter is still getting ready. I'm very grateful for your help with her festival preparations, especially considering you're in the middle of your own ceremony as well. I fear that needing outside assistance means I am lacking as a father."

"Please don't let it bother you. I made a rather eccentric request myself."

Her "request" was one of the things she'd gotten Arnold to agree to the night before. Realizing what she meant, the duke smiled and said, "Ah, yes. It wasn't eccentric. I was very glad you asked."

"I appreciate you agreeing so readily. She might be surprised when she finds out, though."

A sulky voice rose from behind the door. "Papa, Lady Rishe, what are you two talking about?"

"Nothing, dear. Why don't you come out already? You're making Lady Rishe wait."

Millia didn't respond.

The duke sighed. "Are you listening, Millia? This is why I said we should have a maid come with us. It takes too long for you to get ready by yourself."

"I can put a dress on by myself! I put it on just fine."

"Then come out already. It's almost time for rehearsal."

"Please wait a moment, Your Grace. Could you stand down the hall for a short while?" Rishe had the duke move away from the door and then called through it, "Lady Millia, are you perhaps tending to your hair?"

She heard Millia gasp from behind the door and was confident that she'd guessed correctly. *Reason number thirteen Mistress Millia won't get out of her room in the morning: "Know that on humid days, my fluffy hair gets even fluffier!"*

Rishe schooled her expression and whispered through the door, "If that's the case, please allow me to assist you. Would it be all right if only I entered the room?"

There was a pause as Millia deliberated, and then the door opened just a crack.

Seeing that, the duke's face lit up. "Millia!"

"You can't come in, Papa! Only Lady Rishe can!"

"I apologize, Your Grace. Out of respect for a lady's dignity, please wait a few minutes more."

"Oh..." The duke was momentarily stunned by the rejection. Rishe left him in the hall and entered Millia's room.

She was met with the sight of a half-crying Millia, her pale violet hair a poofy mess around her head. "L-Lady Rishe, I..."

The girl must have been struggling with it for some time. Gnarled violet strands wove through the brush in her small hand. No doubt she'd tried to muscle through and endured much pain as a result.

"What do I do? At this rate, we'll be late to the rehearsal. But I can't show myself to Papa and the archbishop like this!"

"Don't worry. I can fix this."

"But I woke up early and I've been trying this whole time! We're not going to make it!"

There was a tray on her end table with what had been her breakfast. Her soup bowl was empty, but more than half of her bread was still there. She'd likely been struggling so hard, she hadn't finished breakfast. *We'll have to fix this quickly so she can finish eating.*

Rishe opened her bag and took the three bottles out. "Lady Millia, please open these bottles and smell them."

"Do they smell like flowers?"

"Yes. This has the scent of a lily, this blue one has the scent of an orchid, and this clear one is lilac."

Millia sniffed the bottles. "These smell good. What are they?"

"They're oils for hair care. If we use these, we'll be able to tame that frizz of yours."

"Oil?! Doesn't hair oil smell weirder, though? The ones I've seen have been kind of white too, but these are see-through."

"These are made from the oils of plants, not from animal fat. They don't smell bad when used in long hair, and they don't solidify either."

Most of Rishe's preparations before leaving Galkhein had been for meeting Millia here. She'd not only prepared the stuffed bear she used in her magic trick but also several items Millia had liked in Rishe's life as her maid, like homemade hair oils and hand creams. The three hair oils she'd taken out of her trunk were ones Millia had most often used in her other life.

"Which of these three do you like the most?"

"How do I pick?! I like all of them, but maybe I'm in the mood for lilac right now."

"Hee hee hee. Then let's go with the lilac today. Have a seat."

Rishe had Millia sit in front of her vanity and dumped some of the oil onto her hand. The sweet but mild scent of flowers wafted through the room. She rubbed the oil on her other hand and started working it into Millia's hair from the inside out.

"I've never seen hair oil like this before. Is it popular in Galkhein?"

"No, it's most often used on the eastern continent. It's hard to get a hold of on this one, so I made it myself."

"You *made* this, Lady Rishe?!"

"Yes. It's easy to do if you can find the ingredients, so I can teach you how to make it later." Rishe finished applying the oil and took the brush from Millia. She combed through Millia's tangles, and the unruly locks gradually settled down.

Millia watched the process with sparkling eyes. "Wow! It was so frizzy before!"

"We have a little extra time, so let me put some braids in it. Is that all right with you?"

"Absolutely!" In the mirror, Millia's cheeks flushed. "It feels like back when Mama would do this for me," she added quietly.

She probably hadn't intended to be heard, so Rishe smiled and changed the subject as she braided Millia's beautiful hair. "And how was your dress yesterday?"

"I gave it back to them without putting it on! The measurements were right, and I didn't want to waste time changing into it."

"My. Isn't it better to see it on you so you can adjust the hem and sleeves?"

"But we're dyeing it, aren't we? Even if I think a white dress should be a certain length, that'll surely change if it's pink instead! In that case, it's better if it's finished faster. If we dye it and I don't think it looks right afterward, we can adjust it then!"

"Hee hee hee, I suppose you're right, Lady Millia."

Millia then faced the window while they were talking. Rishe

followed her gaze and found Leo walking through the courtyard. He wasn't headed for the forest, so he must have been doing some chores.

"Do you ever talk to Leo, Lady Millia?"

"I don't want to talk to him. I mean, he treats me like a child."

"But you're a year younger than him, right?"

"Oh? It's not the years you've lived that determine your maturity, it's your experiences!" Though she was saying things that sounded wise beyond her years, Millia was swinging her legs in her chair in a rather childlike manner. She then hung her head, looking gloomy. "Papa didn't hesitate at all to take him out of the orphanage."

Rishe tilted her head, sensing sorrow and loneliness in Millia's words.

"Papa suddenly brought Leo home one day as a servant. Schneider asked him to 'cause he was in an orphanage run by the Church and he was starting fights every day."

"Is that what happened?"

"Papa brought this kid home with him without even asking me, and you know what he said? He said, 'Leo will play with you. And I want you to learn that there are children with all sorts of circumstances in the world.'"

Rishe thought she could see where Millia's irritation was coming from.

"When I told my maids about this, they said, 'How mean of the master. He should have at least brought a girl to be your friend!' and 'He should have thought of your feelings more,

Mistress Millia,' and 'Why didn't he just get a puppy?' But that's not what I'm mad about. What upsets me is—"

"That what *Leo* wanted wasn't considered at all?"

Millia's eyes went wide as saucers.

"No matter the circumstances of his birth, he should live his own life. He shouldn't have been made your friend or a lesson about the world for you. But you were all anyone was concerned about, and you didn't like that, right?"

"Um, yeah." Millia blinked. "That's right." She considered her words for a moment before continuing, "I hated that. Why did Papa take him just because he was in an orphanage? Maybe he had his own reasons for starting all those fights too. But since Papa didn't say anything to me before taking him in, I couldn't imagine he'd asked Leo what he wanted either."

"I would like to agree with you, Lady Millia, but you know that you weren't completely in the right, don't you?" Rishe asked, and Millia winced.

"You mean getting mad at Papa all the time without explaining my feelings to him?"

"Yes. You didn't explain your feelings to your father yesterday or today, did you, Lady Millia? Why didn't you tell him there was something that made you angry and you weren't just throwing a tantrum?"

"..."

"You were so honest with me. Is there a reason you can't be that honest with your father?"

Millia's expression clouded even more.

This won't do. She's not going to tell me. Rishe sensed Millia wasn't going to confide in her yet, so she gave up on that line of questioning and picked up a lemon-colored ribbon.

"How does this look, Lady Millia?"

"Wow! It's wonderful!" Millia sounded thrilled when she saw herself in the mirror. Rishe had bound the hair on the side of her head in two high, small loops resembling the ears of a bear cub. Under those, she braided the rest of her hair around the back of her head, where she'd tied a ribbon. It was a simple but cute style that suited Millia very well. "What is this? It's so cute!"

I know you liked your hair like this when you were younger, Mistress. Remembering days from her fourth life brought a smile to Rishe's face. As Millia grew older, she stopped fussing for her hair to be done this way, but at ten, she was thrilled about it.

"Thank you, Lady Rishe! Now I know the rehearsal will go great!"

"Tee hee, we should get going, then. Your father's still waiting in the hall. Can you give him a big smile when you go greet him?"

"Why, I can't do that! I must greet him elegantly, like a lady, to match my hairstyle!" Millia pumped herself up and scurried to the door.

Rishe followed her, thinking about what she'd have to do next. *There's still plenty for me to do, though I can't let this opportunity pass me by.*

The rehearsal began shortly afterward, and it went smoother than anyone thought it would. Millia followed all the archbishop's instructions and played the part of the royal priestess with solemnity and grace. She completed her walk through the cathedral's nave to the altar with perfect etiquette, thus showing her pious respect for the goddess. When she recited the lengthy psalms with no problems, the bishops were all stunned.

Rishe sat in the back and observed the rehearsal with a smile. *Mistress Millia is a hard worker. I'm sure when she was chosen to stand in for the royal priestess, she started practicing in secret.*

Although Millia wasn't Rishe's mistress in this life, Rishe cheered her on all the same. She felt proud of the girl's accomplishments.

Someone sidled up next to Rishe—it was Schneider. "This is fantastic. The rehearsal is going so well."

"Greetings, Your Excellency." Rishe acknowledged him with a smile. "I apologize for my behavior last night. Prince Arnold was taking so long to return that I just missed him to bits."

"Ah, um, that's quite all right." Schneider grew sheepish, remembering the affair. He cleared his throat and turned back to Millia, who was before the altar. "I apologize for getting you wrapped up in the festival when you're only here for your own ceremony, Lady Rishe."

"Please, think nothing of it."

"We truly appreciate it, really. To be frank, we probably should have chosen someone of a more mature age to serve as royal priestess, but...the priestess's lineage has a certain hair color, you see."

Rishe recalled the mural on the balcony she'd seen the day before.

"We chose Lady Millia to fulfill that aspect of the priestess's appearance, even if she is only performing as a stand-in."

"You're referring to the line in the psalm about a girl with hair the color of flowers."

"I'm surprised to hear you say that. Most common translations of that psalm call her a girl the color of spring."

"Someone told me how that psalm is meant to be read, you see." She kept Arnold's name a secret just in case. That made her curious about something else, however.

I wonder what Prince Arnold thought of that. What are the chances he noticed that *when he read the psalms? Since it's Prince Arnold, there's a chance he realized everything from the get-go. If that's the case, then his expression back then makes a lot more sense.*

While she was deep in thought, Schneider studied her. His eyes were calm, almost lifeless. When Rishe's eyes met his, he smiled and said, "You yourself have a lovely hair color."

Rishe started. Schneider didn't notice, but she was sure that Arnold would have.

"Someone with hair of your shade would have been picked immediately to stand in for the royal priestess. It's a shame you weren't born in the Holy Kingdom of Domana."

"In a ceremony devoted to the goddess, faith and passion are of paramount importance," Rishe replied with a smile, and Schneider's eyes nearly popped out. "Wouldn't you say, Your Excellency?"

"You're...absolutely right."

"Lady Millia is taking her duty very seriously. If I can help her complete her task in any way, I consider that a great honor."

Schneider had gone quiet, so now it was Rishe's turn to question him.

"If you'll allow me to change the subject, you said something rather strange yesterday, Your Excellency. Why did you tell me not to marry Prince Arnold?"

"Er, perhaps we could discuss that at a later time, somewhere more—"

"Lady Rishe!" Millia trotted down the cathedral's nave.

Schneider's face slackened in surprise before he bowed his head and excused himself. As he left, Rishe watched him carefully. She caught Millia when she leaped into her arms.

"Guess what, Lady Rishe? I didn't make a single mistake in my rehearsal!"

"You didn't? That's impressive, Lady Millia!" Rishe embraced her, and the girl's cheeks reddened as she giggled.

"I have to keep practicing, though!" Millia said enthusiastically. "I mean, this dress isn't the one I'll be wearing for the ceremony, and we didn't use any of the sacred tools! Since the real thing will be a little different, I'll work hard so I can do it perfectly! I must be careful with the sacred tools, after all."

"Ah, yes, the bow and arrows the royal priestess wields. On behalf of the goddess, she must shoot arrows with the power of each season in order for the cycle to continue. Isn't that right?"

"Yep. Although during the festival, she only *mimes* shooting."

The bow may have been a ritual tool, but it was still a weapon. Millia seemed a tad nervous about the prospect of handling it. Rishe squeezed her small hands, wishing to comfort her.

"Shall we dine together, Lady Millia? I arranged for us to have a special lunch in the courtyard."

"You mean a picnic?!"

"That's right. The weather is nice, so I'm sure it'll be fun. The sun might be a bit bright, though, so you should wear a hat." Having been the girl's maid in another life, Rishe couldn't help saying such things. She worried it might come off as strange, but Millia appeared unbothered.

"I've never eaten outside before!"

Rishe beamed at Millia's innocent excitement, but the girl's expression crumpled once Rishe brought her to the site of their midday meal.

***

"Wh...wh-why...?"

When they arrived in the courtyard and Millia saw the blanket laid out on the grass, she stopped in her tracks and began to tremble.

Rishe had been expecting this reaction, so she paid it no mind and began preparing their picnic. Then she invited Millia to join her on the blanket. "Come, Lady Millia. Please sit."

"Wait, Lady Rishe! Tell me why he—" She jabbed her finger at the other person on the blanket. "Tell me why *Leo's* here!"

"I'm not here because I want to be, Mistress Millia," Leo grumbled.

"It's rude to point, Lady Millia," Rishe gently chided her, setting plates upon the blanket. "Can't we enjoy our nice lunch in peace?"

"Well, I didn't know Leo was going to be here! Why is he eating with us?!"

"You were concerned for him just this morning, were you not?"

"But...but this is so sudden! I'm not ready! And Leo, you never eat with us no matter how many times Papa invites you!"

Sulking, Leo replied, "Again, I didn't want to come. I'm just here because I heard I'd get to eat tasty meat."

Millia was shocked. "Y-you're here for meat?!"

This was all part of Rishe's plan. In her life as a knight, Leo was always aloof, but he warmed up a bit whenever they had barbecues in the courtyard.

"Please sit, Lady Millia. If you don't eat quickly, you won't make it in time for your afternoon practice."

"Ugh..." Millia plopped down on the blanket with reluctance.

Rishe opened the basket and brought out the lunch the monks had prepared for them. There were big round buns split in half and stuffed with a meat patty and some vegetables, then covered in a tangy sauce. Very few dishes or utensils were required, making these the perfect picnic food. They would've been familiar to commoners, but Millia had never seen them before.

"Meat and vegetables in such a large piece of bread... H-how does one eat something like this?"

"You hold the bottom half with the wrapping paper and bite off the top. Be careful not to spill the sauce."

"You eat it just like this?!"

Rishe nodded, and Millia timidly opened her mouth.

Leo piped up, "If you keep trying to be proper, you'll just end up nibbling the bread."

"Hmph! It's my first time seeing such food!"

"Hmph." Leo said nothing more. Instead, he opened his mouth wide—making sure Millia could see him—and took a bite of his food.

Millia watched him, stunned. "Your mouth is so big!" Eventually, she eyed the food in her hands and, steeling herself, opened her mouth. Then she took a big bite. At first, she was timid, only chewing a little bit, but after a few seconds, her eyes lit up. "Mmm!"

Evidently, she liked it. Rishe chuckled to see such a transparent reaction. Leo must have been amused too because he covered his mouth as if to hold in a laugh. "I'm glad you like it. Are you enjoying it too, Leo?"

"It's all right."

"Good!" Rishe sighed with relief and began to eat. She'd been worried about throwing Millia and Leo together, but they slowly warmed up to one another.

"Wh-what's that sauce you put on your meat, Leo?"

"I dunno. I wanted to try it 'cause it looked spicy."

"Huh? How could it taste good if it's spicy?"

"I don't think a child could understand, so you probably shouldn't try."

"I'm only a year younger than you!"

They would probably object if Rishe said as much, but the children were having a decently cordial conversation.

I still can't tell how Leo might end up with his injuries. I'm curious about Mistress Millia's "curse" too, but if it's what I'm imagining, then it can't hurt to improve their relationship.

Yesterday, Millia revealed she had the power to curse people. Those she rejected had been endangered. Rishe had to determine why Millia would think she could curse people before dismissing the idea.

Millia interrupted Rishe's thoughts by asking, "Um, er, are you having any problems living with us, Leo?"

"Not really. Other than my employer's daughter throwing crazy tantrums."

"Why, you...!"

"Don't be mean, Leo," Rishe said.

Leo tossed the last of his bread and meat into his mouth, chewed, and swallowed. "I have my own room, and when I'm done with work, I can do whatever I want. In that sense, it's better than when I was at the orphanage."

Millia sagged in relief. With more than half of her lunch still in her hands, she then asked, "What was your orphanage like?"

"Are you asking just 'cause you're curious?"

"N-no! I just want to know." Millia hung her head, and Leo looked a little guilty.

He averted his gaze. "I'd say it was different for everybody there. For anyone who was good at being there, it was probably pretty comfortable."

"And you weren't good at it, so you were chased out and came to live with us instead?"

Leo harrumphed, then added something in such a quiet whisper that Rishe had to read the movement of his lips to know his words: "I had to leave because I *was* good at it."

What could he mean? Rishe was curious, but she didn't want to interrupt their conversation. She ate her lunch in silence as she listened to Leo and Millia talk.

"Bishop Schneider ran the orphanage, right? So is he like a father to you, Leo?"

"Of course he isn't." Leo's curt reply startled the girl. "I owe him. He taught me how to live, but that's all. I don't have any parents."

"I-I'm sorry for saying something so strange. You're not blood-related, so I shouldn't have compared him to a father."

"That's right. I'm done with my lunch. Can I go?"

"Oh, Leo! Wait, wait!" Rishe spoke up.

Leo made a weird face, half standing from the blanket. "What? I need to clean up before I start my afternoon work."

"Your work this afternoon will be different. I asked His Grace if I could borrow you."

"Huh?"

Rishe beamed as Leo grimaced at her.

***

The early afternoon found Rishe in the courtyard on the edge of the Grand Basilica with Leo and Arnold.

"This is Duke Jonal's servant, Leo, whom I told you about last night."

When Arnold fixed his eyes on Leo, the boy blanched. Rishe felt a little bad for him, but he would have to get used to it.

"And Leo, let me reintroduce you. This is..." Rishe peeked at Arnold, who appeared extremely reluctant. She tried not to let it bother her and turned back to Leo again. "This is His Highness Prince Arnold, crown prince of Galkhein."

Leo's knees gave out, and he muttered, "Why is this happening?"

"Say, Leo." The boy raised his head and met Rishe's eyes warily. The one-eyed future version of him had also glared at adults like this. She smiled at the memory and asked, "How would you like to learn martial arts from Prince Arnold?"

"Huh?!" Leo's voice was equal parts surprised and frightened. He gaped at Arnold, blinking at the prince like he couldn't believe what he was hearing. When he saw that Arnold wasn't correcting Rishe (though he did look displeased), he paled again. "Martial arts? Me?!"

"He's really strong, you know. In the last war, he took out a whole company of knights all by himself."

"I know tha—oops!" Leo's hand shot to his mouth, worried that his outburst had been rude. Arnold didn't seem to care, but Leo still felt like he was in trouble.

I'm so glad Prince Arnold agreed to this.

Rishe had proposed the idea the night before. Arnold had wanted to apologize to her, so she had gotten him to agree to three favors. The first had been allowing her to assist with the festival preparations, and this had been the second. *Duke Jonal readily agreed as well. The rest is up to Leo.*

She shot a glance at Arnold, and he seemed to pick up on her intentions.

"Stand," he coldly instructed Leo. Arnold's voice was dispassionate but carried well. He knew how to use it to great efficiency. Whenever he gave an order, it spurred the listener to perk up and carry out his instructions.

Leo was still visibly bewildered, but he pushed himself up. He straightened his spine and met Arnold's gaze.

"Hmph." Arnold narrowed his eyes slightly. "Walk a few steps in any direction."

"Y-yes, sir." Leo trooped a few slow steps around the courtyard.

"Stop."

He came to a quick halt.

Arnold furrowed his brow and turned his head. "Rishe."

"Oh, did you notice as well, Your Highness?"

Rishe tilted her head, and Arnold didn't even try to hide his annoyance as he said, "What did you go and pick this whelp up for?"

"Well, I didn't think I could do anything about it, but I was sure you would be able to, Your Highness."

"You were, were you?" Arnold scowled and closed his eyes, sighing softly.

Leo was openly suspicious, but he still voiced his doubts clearly. "Can someone please explain what's going on?"

"I'm sorry, Leo. Maybe my concern is unwanted, but I just couldn't help worrying about you." Rishe chose her words carefully and asked him, "You're undergoing some kind of training, aren't you?"

Leo's eyes nearly popped out of his head. "Wha—how did you...?"

"You're being pretty reckless about it too. Am I right in saying that you've injured yourself, but rather than allowing it to heal, you're pushing yourself to keep training?"

"Why would you think that?!"

"Your body's movements tell me so."

The boy's strawberry-colored eyes swam with uncertainty.

"It seems like there's no pain anymore, but your right ankle has become weaker. You have a very particular way of walking because you're unconsciously compensating for it. I'm guessing it's easy for you to twist that ankle, but it doesn't hurt much when it happens, yes?"

Leo winced. Though Arnold was silent, he seemed to be of the same opinion. Rishe had walked through the forest with Leo before she noticed, but all Arnold had to do was watch him take a few steps. He must have had formidable powers of observation to have picked up on it so quickly.

"Then there's your arms. Your shoulders, more precisely. You're overusing your right shoulder, aren't you?"

"I..."

"It will affect your growth if things continue this way."

Leo's situation in the future when Rishe had known him was slightly different. His body had been battered in several places, and he'd lost his eye due to a harsh beating that his "previous employer" had given him. His limbs had been injured as well, and he'd had some difficulty moving them at times.

"It's not too late now."

Rishe was remembering her sixth loop. When she and the other knights trained in the courtyard together, Leo would often watch them even though he took every other opportunity he could to avoid people. *Leo wasn't watching* us *back then; he was just watching people practice their swordplay.*

He had clearly yearned to participate. His gaze had been that of someone watching a dream they could never achieve, something he was no longer capable of doing. Rishe wanted to make it so that he never had to look at something that way again in this life.

I don't know what causes Leo to lose an eye after this. Changing his environment is the best way to avoid that, but there's no point in an alternative route that he himself doesn't want to follow. The path one chooses to walk in life should always be a hopeful one, and it should be based on one's own will.

So Rishe thought as she looked up at Arnold. "Well, Your Highness?"

Oliver had also injured himself by training too hard. At Arnold's behest, changes were implemented in the knight cadets' training to lessen the strain on their bodies.

"I won't go against what you've asked of me. What matters most right now is what *he* chooses." Arnold stared Leo down. "If you have the resolve, I'll give you a foothold toward the strength you seek. But I have no intention of lending my aid to someone who lacks that resolve."

"I, um..."

"Your employer has permitted whatever you choose. This is your decision to make."

Leo hesitated, still a bit frightened. "If I learn from you, I have to go to Galkhein, right?"

"That's right. It's up to you how much time you want to devote to this, but you'll have to leave Duke Jonal's house at least for a little while."

The boy's head drooped. "I can't go, then."

Arnold looked unimpressed by his response. "Leo, are you sure you don't have any regrets about this?"

"Of course I do." At some point, the fear had disappeared from Leo's expression. Instead, it was replaced by frustration. Leo looked up at Arnold, that frustration burning in his eyes. "So could you please train me at least for the duration of your stay here?!"

"..."

"I'll use what you teach me to make sure I never push myself with my training again. Please!" he said, bowing deeply. His small shoulders quivered.

Arnold's face was impassive as he said, "I'll take some time starting this evening, then."

Leo's head whipped up, wide-eyed.

"I assume that's fine with you, Rishe?"

"Y-yes, of course, Your Highness. While we're staying here, you'll be busy with your duties, though, won't you?"

"The Church has already requested we extend our stay a few days. Apparently, if they're forced to accompany me at the rate that I wish to proceed, they're the ones who won't last."

Ah, he really doesn't take breaks when he works, huh?

The presence of a Church representative was required for any work Arnold had to take care of at the Grand Basilica. It seemed that the pace he'd set was clearly too harsh for them.

Rishe turned her attention to Leo.

"Thank you," Leo said with another sweeping bow.

As relieved as Rishe was, she thought to herself, *He didn't say he didn't* want *to go to Galkhein—he said he* couldn't *go. A strange response in his position.*

Rishe hadn't told him this, but there was something else she'd noticed. There was a good chance Arnold had as well. Now didn't seem like the right time to bring it up, however.

"I'm sorry for springing this on you, Leo."

Leo shot her a sulky look. "You should be. Don't you think you should have explained this to me before bringing me here?"

"I thought you'd run away if I did."

"Any commoner would run if you told them they were going to meet royalty from another country!"

Arnold regarded Rishe as the two of them spoke. "Do you know this kid from somewhere?"

Seriously, you're too perceptive! Rishe shook her head, careful to conceal her internal panic. "No. What gave you that impression?"

"He's awfully casual with you for some servant child."

Tiptoeing around it, she whispered, "That's because he thinks I'm a body double and not really me."

Arnold whirled away from her at once. He seemed as stoic as

always, but he had one large hand clapped over his mouth and his shoulders shook.

"Huh?! Your Highness, are you trying not to laugh right now?!"

"...No."

"You're lying! Hey, look at me!"

As Rishe circled Arnold, Leo reached out to her, flustered. His face was etched with concern, as if she might face consequences as a "body double" for being so frank with the crown prince. It was kind of him to worry.

"If everything's settled, I should be getting back to work."

Arnold totally ignored me!

Still, Rishe had her own work to do. She'd spent her morning helping Millia, so she should use her afternoon for the rest of the suspended ceremony.

This thing with Leo bothers me too. Even if he's going to be under Prince Arnold's tutelage, I can't imagine that will change his future.

Just then, someone approached them in the courtyard.

"Your Highness, Lady Rishe."

"Oh, Oliver."

Oliver bowed and glanced at Leo. He hesitated for a moment, then stood beside Arnold and told him, "I have something to report to the both of you."

"What, me too?" Rishe had a bad feeling about that.

Arnold frowned. "Give us the short version."

"Very well. The festival may be delayed." Oliver sighed. "The seamstresses finishing Lady Millia's dress appear to have fallen ill."

Rishe gasped. "What?!"

It seemed ill fortune beset whatever Millia rejected: first the carriage, and now the white dress.

* * *

"Apparently, the seamstresses have all come down with colds," Duke Jonal said with a strained smile. He was sitting in the room they were using for their festival preparations.

Rishe sat across from him, having rushed there as soon as she heard the news. She took steady, controlled breaths through her nose to conceal her windedness.

The duke shrugged. "They were probably just working too hard with the festival fast approaching. The stress got to them, and they all collapsed at once."

"That's terrible. Can I ask what their symptoms are?"

"From what I hear, they have high fevers and are complaining of fatigue."

Rishe frowned. *That's not good.* She glanced sideways at Leo, who stood in a corner of the room as Duke Jonal's servant. He looked displeased, but it probably had nothing to do with the postponement of his training with Arnold.

Turning to the duke, Rishe asked, "Lady Millia must be upset that her dress won't be finished on time. I'd like to comfort her. May I ask where she is?"

"W-well..." the duke began, hesitant.

"I'm fine, Lady Rishe," came a cute voice from behind him.

"Lady Millia?"

Millia appeared, the very picture of composure. There was a mature calm in her eyes. She was like a different person from the little girl who had been on the verge of tears this morning because her hair was uncooperative.

Two men stood behind her. One was Bishop Schneider, and the other was an old man who wore a symbol on his chest that indicated a higher rank.

Rishe stood and bowed, thinking, *This must be the current archbishop.* The archbishop Rishe knew from her other life was the next one. *I'm not familiar with the archbishop or Bishop Schneider. That would mean the two of them leave the Grand Basilica sometime in the next few years.*

"Lady Rishe." Rishe looked up and Millia was standing before her with a gentle smile on her face. "I've reflected on my actions. It was my selfishness that made the seamstresses overwork themselves."

"Lady Millia, you..."

"I've sworn to the goddess that I'll be a good girl until the festival. I won't need your assistance anymore."

Rishe blinked.

Next to Millia, the archbishop smiled warmly and said, "Lady Rishe, I apologize as well on behalf of the Church. Given that you are the future empress of Galkhein, we cannot possibly take up any more of your precious time."

"Don't be silly. I enjoyed helping Lady Millia, and I was actually hoping to provide more assistance."

"Thank you, but don't worry about me." Millia's smile was innocent, but it drew a line between them. "I don't need a pink dress. Any dress that can be prepared for me quickly is fine. It's most important that the festival not be delayed! Isn't that right, Bishop Schneider?"

"Yes, Lady Millia. It's exactly as you say."

Rishe knelt to Millia's eye level and said, "Very well, Lady Millia. I won't help with the festival anymore."

The girl looked relieved.

"I just want you to know one thing."

"What is it?"

Rishe remembered the past life they shared together and beamed at her. "I think you're adorable when you're full of energy, and I love you when you're being selfish too."

Millia's honey-colored eyes swam for a moment. Maybe it was just Rishe's imagination, but it looked like she was about to cry. Instead, however, she turned her back on Rishe and looked up at the archbishop. "Your Excellency, Bishop Schneider, we should hurry to evening prayer. It would be rude to the goddess if we were late."

"Yes. Let us go, My Lord Duke."

As they left, Bishop Schneider called out to the boy still waiting in the corner. "What are you doing, Leo? You must attend as well."

"I know." Leo was watching how the scene played out before he sulkily answered the bishop. He stole a glance at Rishe as he passed, but the moment their eyes met, he looked away.

Rishe was alone, but not for long. Oliver soon joined her.

"Lady Rishe, my lord will be coming soon. Would you mind waiting here?"

"He will?"

After they heard about the seamstresses, Rishe and Leo had made way for the basilica. Arnold, meanwhile, received another report from Oliver. Had he already taken care of whatever that had been about?

Eventually, heralded by the *thud* of his hard boots on the floor, Arnold entered the room. He looked at Rishe, frowning. "Oliver, leave us. Continue with what we discussed earlier."

"Very well. Pardon me."

As Oliver left the room, Arnold sat across from Rishe with a scroll in his hand. Still frowning, he asked, "Why the long face?"

"I was trying not to show it." Rishe wore her sadness plain and pressed her hands to her cheeks. "I don't think Lady Millia's doing well. She tried to hide it, but she looked like she was about to cry. She only makes that face when she's pretending to be okay. I'm worried."

Arnold sighed and thrust the scroll toward her. "Open it."

Curious, Rishe undid the binding cord. Once it unfurled, revealing its contents, Rishe gasped. "This is...!"

The first words she saw were "Investigation Report." There was an illustration of a familiar-looking carriage and its various individual parts. The contents confirmed something Rishe already suspected.

I wanted to sneak out of the Basilica and investigate this myself!

In the middle of the page was a drawing bigger than the rest. It was the front wheel of a carriage and the axle connecting it to the vehicle.

"The front wheel of Duke Jonal's crashed carriage was tampered with."

Rishe's heart rate sped up, but it wasn't because of the tampering of the carriage. It was because Arnold had investigated the accident.

"The carriage didn't belong to the Jonal family. They were using it because the day before they departed, that child threw a tantrum about wanting to ride in a white carriage. The duke granted the girl's demand and sent out for a white carriage."

"You suspected it was an accident someone set up and not a curse."

"You didn't?"

Arnold had asked it as though he already knew the answer, but Rishe couldn't respond right away. After all, her personal experience proved that a strange, inexplicable power indeed existed in this world. Something surpassing human understanding happening to someone else didn't seem peculiar to her, since she had redone her own life several times now. Therefore, Rishe couldn't discard the possibility that Millia was experiencing was something similar. At the same time, she understood the chances were low. And now Arnold was showing her evidence of what she already suspected herself: The accident had been caused by human hands.

"I already thought it was odd." Arnold languidly rested his chin in his hand. "Twenty-two years ago, the previous priestess died, and then her younger sister died ten years ago. Because of that, there was no longer anyone who could play the role of the priestess at the festival, so it hasn't been held for the last twenty-two years."

"Yes. The younger sister was of ill health, so she was in no position to take over the role."

That girl had been the last female member of the priestess's bloodline. The only remaining heirs were said to be a handful of men. The festival had been suspended while the Church waited for a girl to be born to the bloodline.

"There's no reason to start using a stand-in now," Arnold stated with certainty. "Holding the festival in name only to appease their followers is nothing more than an excuse. After all, if they truly believe in the existence of the goddess, then a festival with a stand-in is meaningless."

He all but confirmed Rishe's suspicions.

Prince Arnold thought so from the very beginning. Probably from when he first laid eyes on Millia. I didn't think he would find out so soon even if he is the *Prince Arnold...but now that I think about it, he can read the psalms too.*

When she factored in his linguistic knowledge, it didn't surprise her that he also knew the qualifications for the royal priestess.

As if to prove that point, Arnold looked Rishe squarely in the eyes and said, "It's said that the priestess who inherits the goddess's blood has hair the color of flowers."

Millia's hair was a pale violet color. The beautiful color of a flower that bloomed in spring.

"Common knowledge of the psalms doesn't touch on this characteristic of the priestess. They likely translated the text in such a way to make it easier to hide the priestess when they needed to."

"Like they're doing now, you mean?"

"So you *did* notice," he said with some amusement.

Rishe couldn't immediately agree. It wasn't that she had *noticed*—she'd already known for a long time. The memory she found herself recalling now was a confession she'd heard in her fourth life.

"Millia is not my daughter. She was entrusted to me by someone for a very important purpose."

The previous royal priestess left behind a sickly, much younger sister. The woman was not able to succeed her sister's duties and spent most of her life sequestered in a church. She finally gave up that life to give birth to a daughter. Her daughter had been raised in secret, and Rishe herself had lovingly watched over her as she grew up.

Arnold, who knew nothing about that, said matter-of-factly, "That child has the qualifications to be the true priestess."

And that must be the reason...

The prince regarded her like he could see through everything, and Rishe stared right back at him.

...why you tried to kill her in the future.

CHAPTER 4

"I DON'T WANT TO STUDY! I want to eat sweets today, not study!"

In Rishe's life as a maid, sometimes Millia would shout and lock herself up in her room. This was when Rishe grew skilled at lockpicking.

Rishe could tell by the sound of her voice when Millia really wanted to be alone and when she was just craving attention. On this day, it was the latter, so Rishe unlocked the door without hesitation and entered her room. She looked down at the round lump of blankets on the bed.

"You were working so hard up until yesterday, Mistress," Rishe coaxed. She was dressed in a maid uniform with her hair in a ponytail. "You're writing a letter to the archbishop in the Crusade language for the festival next month, aren't you?"

"I didn't want to anymore when I woke up this morning! Boys don't have to learn Crusade, and I can do my job as the royal priestess's stand-in without being able to read the psalms! I'm sick of being the only one who has to study so hard!"

Rishe thought, *I hear it takes* adults *a long time to learn Crusade.*

The girl had been twelve then, and she hadn't yet been told who she really was. Rishe found out first because the duke had opened up to her about it. A year into working there, he had come to her and told her, "I want one person I can trust at Millia's side who knows her secret." Since Millia was the real priestess, she would need to know the Crusade language. But since she was being made to learn it without yet knowing her origins, she was having a hard time of it.

"Mistress Millia," Rishe said, leaning over the bed. "The more knowledge you gain, the more weapons you'll have at your disposal. Or maybe it would be better to say that knowledge will expand your world."

Millia remained curled up, but she was quiet. Contemplative, perhaps.

"If you learn a language most people know nothing about, then you'll get a glimpse into a *world* they know nothing about. Aren't you curious about how the people in myths lived, what sort of dreams they had, and what they found beautiful? There might even be wonderful love poems written by the goddess."

The lump twitched at that. Millia happened to be experiencing a bout of puppy love.

"In fact, I wish I could participate in your lessons on Crusade as well."

"You do?"

"Yes! Why, I would be ecstatic if you would be my teacher, Mistress Millia."

Millia sprang up, her covers piling in front of her with a soft *whump*. She regarded Rishe with sparkling eyes. "You'll come and study with me, Rishe?"

"Of course. You'll have to learn a lot by yourself first, though."

"I'll do it! It sounds fun, me teaching you!" Millia's mood had completely recovered. She jumped out of bed and gave Rishe an enthusiastic hug.

"I look forward to learning from you. Let's get you ready to go to your lessons, Mistress Millia."

"Yes! I might see Lord Bernhard, so make sure I'm extra cute today, all right?"

"Hee hee hee. As you say, Mistress."

After this exchange, Millia engaged with her studies diligently and began to teach Rishe what she'd learned later that day. That was why Rishe was able to read Crusade. She'd even traveled with Millia to the Grand Basilica and exchanged words with the archbishop at the time. But all of that had occurred in a different lifetime.

***

I never found out the reason why Mistress Millia's identity as the true royal priestess was kept hidden from the world, but I feel like I might have an idea now.

That evening, Rishe found herself staring down at a pot in the kitchen in a distant corner of the Grand Basilica. She was alone with Arnold, boiling a concoction of medicinal herbs. She'd begged him to convince the Church that they be allowed to use the kitchen.

Slowly stirring the pot, she tilted her head back and asked Arnold, who was behind her, "Do you believe in curses, Your Highness?"

If she had to guess, he didn't. In fact, she figured even asking the question was a waste of time, but his answer surprised her.

"There are times when it's convenient to say I do."

Rishe spun on her heel. Arnold was seated at a table, chin in hand and watching Rishe work dispassionately.

"By which you mean…?"

"When it comes to manipulating public opinion, the concept of power surpassing human understanding is useful. It's especially striking on the battlefield; such things can significantly influence soldiers' morale."

"I see." She'd been caught off guard at first, but his explanation was just what she'd expect of him. It was less about what he himself believed and more about applications in tactics and politics.

"The duke likely believes in this 'curse' his daughter possesses. Since the girl is the real priestess, he must think it only natural that she could possess such a power."

"You're probably right. His denial of the curse's existence seemed more for my benefit than anything else."

Duke Jonal must've been trying to prevent her from guessing at Millia's identity.

"If it were just the carriage accident, that would be one thing, but with this seamstress incident as well, he wanted to keep you away before you caught on."

Is that the only reason he didn't want me helping with the festival? Rishe stepped back from the pot, took out some small bottles from her bag, and set them on the table.

"What are these?"

"Poisons I collected yesterday," Rishe answered matter-of-factly, and Arnold barked a laugh.

"Well, this is a lot more interesting than a stuffed bear."

"I found several traps set up in the forest around the Grand Basilica. I wiped them with my handkerchief, soaked it in water, and isolated the poison through precipitation."

In the bottle on the right, the poison had sunk to the bottom. In the left, it floated near the top.

"The bottle on the left contains a sleeping drug that takes effect immediately. This amount could put a grown man to sleep in a few minutes. Hunters normally use it."

Arnold thought back to a past incident. "You said something similar when bandits attacked us on our way back to Galkhein from your homeland. Back then, it was a drug that caused paralysis, but you said it was used in a similar way."

"Yes. It's all because meat quality suffers if prey is too active before its death. Though if the poison is so concentrated that it kills its prey instantly, the meat will suffer for another reason—the failure to drain the animal's blood promptly after death. Hence, these drugs are used to keep animals alive and relaxed in their traps until the hunter can come collect them."

She picked up the bottle and shook it. "Both that paralysis drug and this sleeping drug lose their toxicity if exposed to heat. However, this drug has another special property."

"Let's hear it."

Rishe set that bottle down and flicked her eyes to the other. "The poison in the bottle on the right seems to be lethal." It contained a transparent poison with a slight tinge of red. "If a lethal dose is ingested, it's a matter of minutes till death. If you ingest less than that, you'll immediately experience high fever and lethargy, and you will be incapacitated for around a week."

"..."

"This poison has an interesting interaction with the sleeping drug here. The two counteract each other."

Arnold frowned. "They counteract?" he asked, and she nodded.

"The sleeping drug neutralizes the poison. Likewise, the poison prevents the sleeping drug from taking effect." She pressed the two bottles on the table together with a *clink*. "If you ingest these two drugs at the same time, you will neither fall asleep nor die."

"You'll just go on like nothing happened?"

"Yes. But your body will fully absorb the sleeping drug in a matter of hours, neutralizing its effect. At that time, only the poison will remain in your system."

"So you can die hours after ingesting the poison for seemingly no reason," Arnold noted.

"The only reasons you'd use poison when hunting are if you were trying to catch a particularly ferocious beast or if you only had access to less potent weapons. I didn't see any signs of dangerous creatures in the forest, so I can't think of a reason for coating those traps with these poisons."

"But hunters would only use bows, right? Things like bows and throwing knives aren't very powerful. If it's difficult to kill animals with those weapons alone, doesn't it stand to reason that they'd also use poisons?"

"The thing is, this poison isn't neutralized by heat like the other one. The only thing it has going for it is that it wouldn't make the animal suffer needlessly, thus keeping the pelt undamaged. But the sleeping drug should be no different on that front." There was another doubt Rishe harbored. "Both poisoned traps smelled like metal as well."

She'd noticed when she was sniffing the poisons coated on the traps the day before.

"Animals have a strong sense of smell. Normally, hunters will bury new traps in the soil for months or submerge them in river water to eliminate their scent so that animals won't notice them. There's no way someone would set up a trap that I could smell on my handkerchief and expect to catch anything with it."

"Their aim is clear, then." Arnold leaned back in his chair and said calmly, "The trap was set not for an animal but for a human."

Rishe said nothing in response. In truth, she'd been hoping for him to pronounce her idea as ludicrous. If Arnold agreed with her, however, then she had to be firm in her conviction.

"Bluntly put, it's an assassination tool. If someone went into the forest and triggered the trap, they would think it was a simple injury."

"Yes," she said. "They would return to the Basilica and, by the time their wounds had been treated, they would simply die a painless death."

"If it were a fast-acting poison, they would suffer the effects as soon as they were injured. They'd notice the poison immediately, and someone else would probably be able to suck it out of the wound."

"Right, though I can't recommend trying to suck out a poison this deadly. Even if you spit it out immediately, it would still be putting poison in your mouth. I wouldn't be surprised if it killed the person attempting to treat the poison as well."

Such methods should only be taken for paralyzing or sleeping drugs. Rishe's master in her life as an apothecary had said so, and Rishe firmly believed the same thing herself.

"I take it you're whipping up an antidote in that pot?"

"Yes. I was able to find the herbs that make up the base for the sleeping drug in the forest nearby. It's not the best time of year for them, so I was only able to make enough for five people."

Sensing Rishe's intentions, Arnold let out a sigh. "Oliver can deliver it to the four seamstresses."

"Thank you, Your Highness!" Rishe was relieved to hear it, but she couldn't be entirely optimistic yet.

Arnold seemed to share the sentiment. "You said fatigue and fever would only occur when given a nonlethal dosage of the poison. It sounds like that's what happened to the seamstresses."

"I believe they absorbed it through their skin instead of ingesting it or receiving it through a wound." And there was only one thing the four seamstresses were guaranteed to have touched. "I believe Lady Millia's dress was coated in the same compound of poisons."

This morning, Millia had told her she was so looking forward to dyeing the dress that she'd sent for it to be adjusted without trying it on to get it back faster.

"A fatal dose for a young child would be smaller than one for a grown woman. If Lady Millia had tried on the dress yesterday, she would have been poisoned and could have died." The image of Millia dead pushed aside the memory of her letting Rishe brush her hair and being delighted by the ribbon. A chill scuttled down Rishe's spine.

"All because I convinced her to try on the dress," Rishe said quietly, willing her voice to keep steady. One false step and the worst could have happened.

While she was consumed by the thought, Arnold said, "Don't be scared of a future you've only imagined."

Rishe's shoulders jumped. "Your Highness..."

He still sounded disinterested, but his words were firm. Arnold looked Rishe right in the eye and continued, "Don't get them confused. What you've imagined is only a possibility; it's not the reality."

Rishe's breath caught.

"What you fear has not actually occurred."

He was right; the worst-case scenario had already been avoided. Rishe took a deep breath.

"The same goes for the seamstresses. Regardless of your actions, they would have begun work on their final adjustments."

"..."

"Rishe."

She nodded at his urging. "I understand. I'd like to deliver the antidote to the seamstresses as quickly as possible."

"Good," Arnold said, appraising.

Although she felt her brows droop, this was no time to feel down.

What are *Prince Arnold's plans for Mistress Millia?*

Rishe truly felt that the Arnold sitting in front of her now was a kind person. But the plan he harbored in his heart was so important to him that carrying it out would crush that kindness into dust.

That was why, five years from now, Arnold mobilized the military to kill Millia. Since someone was clearly after Millia's life now and Rishe was trying to protect her, she had no idea what sort of actions Arnold would take in response. It was more than possible that he would oppose her.

Mustering up her courage, Rishe said, "I'd like to tell Duke Jonal that someone is trying to assassinate Lady Millia. If we're going to protect her, we'll need the approval of her legal guardian."

He lowered his gaze thoughtfully. "You're right. That'll probably be more effective than telling him to worry about a curse."

Relieved, Rishe stood from her chair. "I'll have the antidote finished by the time they're done with their prayers. If you wouldn't mind, please arrange for it to be administered."

"I got it."

Rishe rolled up her sleeves and returned to the pot, which had just finished boiling. She confirmed the state of the antidote and transferred it into five small bottles. She wanted to cool it under some running water first, but she needed to get it to the seamstresses as soon as possible. She entrusted the bottles to Arnold and hoped the brew would cool enough during transport.

"All right, I'll head to the building with the guest lodgings."

"Right. I'll order Oliver to deliver this as fast as he can."

"Thank you, Your Highness." With a deep parting curtsy to Arnold, Rishe strode in the opposite direction. When she arrived at the other building, she went up to the floor that housed the duke and his daughter's rooms and waited for them there.

Maybe I should have headed for the cathedral where they're praying, but I need to be cautious. She'd come here instead because she couldn't trust Schneider and the other bishops. *For now, I should only tell Duke Jonal about my suspicions. If he would allow it, I'd like to protect Mistress Millia at all times.*

Easier said than done, considering the clergymen had indirectly asked Rishe keep her distance. She wouldn't be able to stay with Millia without drawing the Church's attention.

Maybe I should fake an assassination attempt on myself as well and just get them to increase all-around security in the Basilica? No, they'll just tell me to return to Galkhein where I'll be safe.

Time ticked by while Rishe considered her options. *They're a little late getting back, aren't they?*

Right then, she heard small footsteps coming her way. She thought it was Millia, but she quickly amended herself. *Those are Leo's footsteps.*

Just as she suspected, it was Leo. He scrambled up the stairs toward her, out of breath and flustered. "Did Mistress Millia come here?!"

Surprised, Rishe shook her head. "No, she's not back yet. Is she missing?"

Leo's face fell. "After prayer, the adults had something to talk about back in the cathedral, so I was told to escort her to her room. On our way, the wind snatched her ribbon. She looked like she was gonna cry, so I went after it by myself, and while I was gone, well..."

"No..." Rishe felt that chill creep up her spine once more. She didn't want to scare Leo, but she couldn't help panicking as she asked, "Was anyone approaching just before you left her?"

"No, no one. I'm sure there was no one nearby, but..."

"But?"

"While we were walking, she asked me where the orphanage I grew up in was. I told her it was just past the woods to the east."

Everything clicked for Rishe in that moment.

"I was hoping she went back to her room without me."

Millia *hadn't* just gone back to her room like she was supposed to, Rishe was sure of that. "Please, Leo. Can you run back to the cathedral and tell people you trust about this? If possible, I'd like it if you could tell Prince Arnold too. He should be somewhere near the administration building."

"But I have to go search for her in the fores—"

"I'll go to the forest!" It would be safer for Rishe to search for Millia, on account of the traps. She had to find her before anything happened to her. "Please!"

Rishe ran off without waiting for Leo to answer her. As the setting sun dyed the Grand Basilica crimson, she dashed through the eastern halls. She reached the forest before the area fell into complete darkness.

A child's footprints—and they're not Leo's. These are girls' shoes! Rishe grimaced, her breathing shallow. *I knew it. Mistress Millia went into the forest.*

She itched to surge forward, let her panic lead the way, but she'd miss vital clues if she did that. As she caught her breath, she scanned the forest. There wasn't a lot of exposed dirt, and much of the ground was covered in fallen leaves. Only a few footprints dotted the area, but Rishe walked straight in without hesitation. The footprints were oriented east; she was confident Millia had gone in that direction. She paid attention to whatever small traces she might find, be it new tracks in the soil, oddly parted grass, spiderwebs torn a certain way, branches broken by a shoe or a hoof or fall, or whatever else.

Humans were awfully large compared to most animals, a fact Rishe tended to forget. Even a child such as Millia was larger and heavier than the vast majority of woodland animals. That was why she had ample clues to follow.

Calm down, stay cool, and don't make a mistake. Leave traces for whoever Prince Arnold sends after us.

She pressed forward, noticing the difference between marks left by a large animal and ones left by a human child.

If I make a mistake, I could be too late!

A terrible premonition welled up in her, but she quashed it with a deep breath. Eventually, she came upon some violet hair caught on tree bark. Relieved as she was to be heading in the right direction, a new anxiety arose in her.

I only came this far with Leo. I don't know what sort of traps may lay ahead.

At that moment, she sensed a presence that didn't belong to an animal.

I found her!

Rishe spotted a small girl some distance away. Without a doubt, it was Millia. She was seated against the base of a tree, rubbing her eyes with the backs of her hands over and over again. Rishe's heart wrenched at the sight.

"Lady Millia!"

Millia flinched, then turned toward her. She must have been crying all by herself in this dark forest.

Rishe rushed to her. "Are you hurt?!"

"Oh, Lady Rishe!" Millia reached out and clung to her.

"Does anything hurt? Did you twist your ankle or injure yourself?" Millia shook her head. Rishe stroked her hair, relieved to hear it. "Thank goodness."

The girl swallowed her sobs and mustered a shaky question: "Why are you so nice to me?"

"What do you mean?"

"I have a bad power! It'll put you in danger too, Lady Rishe."

Rishe blinked and studied her. She really did look to be

on the verge of tears. "I was under the impression that you liked me."

"O-of course I do! I really like you!"

"Hee hee, I'm happy to hear it. Doesn't that mean I'll be safe even if you *can* curse people?"

Millia hung her head, tiny shoulders trembling. "But Mama died back then!" Big droplets spilled from her honey-colored eyes. "One day, I got in a lot of trouble, and I yelled, 'I hate you, Mama!' That night, Mama collapsed, and she never came back after that." Millia's face twisted in agony. "I have such a bad power. I went and said that, even though I really love her! It's all my fault she died!"

In Rishe's life as a maid, Millia had never said much about her mother's death. She'd always looked like she didn't want to talk about it, so Rishe made a point not to bring it up. This was Rishe's first time seeing how deeply the tragedy wounded her.

"Y-you know, Rishe..." The words poured out of Millia in concert with her tears. Once she started to speak, it was like the dam holding back her feelings had broken. "I was trying to get Papa to hate me. If I could leave Papa, then what happened to Mama wouldn't happen to him, right?"

"You—"

"I decided to be selfish—to be a bad girl. If Papa started hating me, he'd send me back to the orphanage!" Millia sniffled, rubbing her eyes again and again. Her voice trembled after rejecting her father so many times. "I love Papa, but if he'll die because of me, then it'd be better if he hated me and got rid of me. I don't care if I can't be with him anymore, I just want him to be okay."

"Goodness, Lady Millia..."

"Up until now, it's been okay. When I wasn't actually mad, I could say I hated something, and the curse wouldn't happen. But the carriage yesterday and the dress today...all of it was my fault."

Rishe gently took Millia's hand before she could rub her eyes again. "That's why you said you'd stop being selfish earlier."

Millia gave a little nod.

The Church didn't have anything to do with that, then. It was a decision Millia came to after doing her best to come up with a way no one else would get hurt.

"My real Mama and Papa probably threw me away because they didn't want a cursed child. Bishop Schneider must have asked Papa to take me in like he did with Leo, and that's when I started living with him."

Suddenly, Rishe understood why Millia had told Leo *"You're not blood-related, so I shouldn't have compared him to your father"* at lunch earlier that day. Her tone was uncharacteristically cold even though she was supposedly speaking of Leo and Schneider. But she hadn't meant them. She had been reflecting on herself.

She already knew she wasn't her father's daughter. Evidently, the girl was trying to tell herself that there should be more distance between her and the duke.

"Papa is so kind. He raised me even though I'm not really his child, and if I really want to give all my love back to him, then I can't just wait for him to get rid of me."

"So you asked Leo where the orphanage was and decided to leave on your own?"

"Ugh..." Millia looked up at Rishe and wailed, "I'm sorry for throwing away the ribbon you tied for me, Lady Rishe!"

Rishe just wrapped her arms around Millia and hugged her tight. "I should be the one apologizing, Lady Millia."

The girl hiccupped and wailed, her little body racked with sobs.

"You looked so sad sometimes, but I couldn't even reach out and comfort you to the very end."

She should never have left Millia alone with her sadness. When she pouted and said that she wanted to be left alone, Rishe should have embraced her and asked what was troubling her.

"You've been fighting all this time to protect your father."

Another loud wail tore free from the girl's lips.

"You're a wonderful girl, Lady Millia. If you leave your father, he will be so sad that he'll cry."

"H-he will?"

Millia sounded like she couldn't even imagine it, so Rishe smiled and nodded. She'd seen it herself on the night before Millia's wedding. Duke Jonal had been a sobbing mess. Whether they were blood relations meant nothing to him.

"Let's go back to your father, Lady Milla."

But Millia still shook her head. "No, I can't go back!"

"Oh, come now..."

"I don't want to be near anyone I love! It shouldn't have to be Papa or Mama. *I* should die before anyone else!"

"Wait!"

Millia shoved Rishe with all her might, and Rishe heard something click. It was a hard sound, like something striking metal. Rishe's eyes reflexively darted to Millia's feet. That's when she noticed the thin string hooked around the heel of one of Millia's shoes.

Oh no!

Rishe only had a split second to think.

The reason Millia was crying here, the metallic sound from up high... If Millia tripped on something, what traps might use a string? Wasn't there a trap I saw in her past life that used a tripwire to determine its target's location? Ah! A poison arrow trap!

"No!" Rishe's hand shot out. She grabbed Millia by the shoulder and threw herself on top of the girl.

The next instant, pain seared through her neck. It burned like fire, but she knew the sensation of heat was just an illusion. Her vision distorted, and she dug her nails in the dirt. She hadn't been able to completely avoid it, and red blood dripped from the scratch.

"No! Lady Rishe!"

The arrow that had grazed Rishe was sticking out of the ground. Rishe recognized the color of the drug coating its arrowhead.

It's the same mixed poison that was on the other traps! Rishe grit her teeth and cupped her neck. Her fingers slipped on the blood. *I was grazed, that's all. If I'm only bleeding this much from a neck wound, the actual cut isn't anything to worry about. The problem is...*

The poison compound that had entered her bloodstream.

Rishe grunted as her thoughts warped. She felt faint. It was a slight relief, however, that she recognized what she was feeling as a powerful drowsiness. *The nectar poison hasn't taken effect yet.*

There was a fast-acting sleeping drug mixed into this poison that counteracted its effects. Until her body completely absorbed the sleeping drug, it would stave off the effects of the poison. At present, the only symptom Rishe felt was drowsiness, not nausea or pain.

They're not negating one another...the sleeping drug is overpowering the poison. This compound must contain more of the... first one.

She needed to think of a way out of this situation, but her thoughts were fragmented. She crouched on the ground, desperately trying to string them together. Drops of blood fell to the soil.

Millia quaked with fear, but she managed to stand and yelled, "J-just wait, Lady Rishe! I'll go get someone!"

"No...you mustn't...go out on your own!" Rishe could hardly breathe, and she couldn't raise her voice enough to be heard. As she listened to Millia's footsteps fade into the distance, she cursed her own failure.

How could you make a mistake like this? Showing Mistress Millia your blood and making her worry so?

She couldn't let herself become another reason for Millia's anguish. The girl was so young. Rishe should have been looking out for more than just her physical safety—she should've protected Millia's heart as well.

You can't sleep. Stay conscious, do something, buy yourself time! Struggle!

Unfortunately, she had no herbs for an antidote, and the ones she *had* created would be on a carriage right about now. All five went to the seamstresses so there would be a spare if anything happened to one of them. It was Rishe's policy to make extras in case of damage or loss during transport. She was sure that *he* had made the arrangements to transport them properly—but, wait, who was that? No, worrying about that could come later.

Ah, the wound... I must at least remove whatever poison is still in my skin around the wound!

The burning, friction-like pain was caused by the poison. After making contact with the skin, the nectar poison would enter the bloodstream in thirty minutes. The more poison that seeped into her body, the more chances she would suffer lasting effects even if she drank an antidote.

I don't have any water, and I can't constrict it or suck it. I've only got one other option!

Rishe was doubled over on the ground now, her forehead pressed to the earth. She reached down to her leg, fingers quivering, and somehow managed to remove the dagger strapped to her thigh. Using both her hands didn't seem feasible at present, so she held the sheath in her mouth to remove the blade.

I have to wash it with new blood.

That was the only method available to her. She carefully attempted to cut her skin, but her fading consciousness was making it hard to aim away from any major arteries.

Her hand suddenly relaxed, and the dagger slipped from her grip. "Ack!"

Pull yourself together! There's no other way to fix this. I can't let my lady's heart be scarred any more than it already has—no, I'm not her maid right now! I must wake Master Hakurei... Wait, was this my third loop?

Her thoughts spun and got muddled in the mess. She exhaled deeply, grasping for the dagger next to her.

Even if Mistress Millia went for help, the people of the Church won't enter the forbidden forest. I must handle this myself! No one will come into the forest if it means getting on the Church's bad side...

Something nagged at her. Rishe sat hunched over on the ground and furrowed her brow. *Why am I thinking of Arnold Hein right now?*

That emperor had declared war on the country that Rishe had served as a knight. She tried to convince herself of this, but the strange feeling in her mind only grew. She had to hurry, but the whole world spun.

Emperor Arnold Hein is King Zahad's enemy... He destroyed Coyolles and executed the royal families of so many nations. That tyrant tried to kill Mistress Millia and His Highness the prince, and he killed my captain and Joel... That cruel man started a world war and let countless people die... He has a real mean streak...

As her wound throbbed, Rishe grew more and more feverish. She planted both hands on the ground and tried to raise her upper body as she continued painting a mental picture of Arnold.

His sword form is beautiful. His posture is always good, and he works efficiently. He faces people sincerely. He's thoughtful and also bold, but sometimes he seems almost cowardly.

She heard a leaf crunch underfoot but found it too difficult to discern more than that. A deep fog shrouded her thoughts, and few things were still clear to her. She could only focus on his black hair and his azure eyes, the color of the sea. His soft voice when he called her name, the feeling of his fingers in her hair. The exasperation plain on his face when he looked her way, and the ever-so-rare smile he showed her and only her.

He always looks straight at me. He's a liar, but he doesn't want to be. He's actually very kind. He's the man I'm going to marry, my...

Rishe raised her head to stare at the person before her. For some reason, she was on the verge of tears.

"My husband..."

Arnold was out of breath. She had never seen him like that before. Scowling, he scanned her and clicked his tongue before grabbing her shoulder roughly. She gasped as he pulled her up and pressed her back to the tree behind her. Gripping her shoulder, Arnold sank his teeth into her bleeding neck.

"Aah!"

Then he sucked, loud and hard. She flinched at the strange sensation and paled a second later. Arnold had his lips on her wound and was draining the poison from it. She stiffened.

"No, w-wait!"

Arnold spat out the blood and drew in a short breath. He brought his lips in close again, and Rishe mustered what strength she could to resist.

"Prince Arnold, y-you mustn't! If you do that, you'll—!"

Arnold ignored her desperate pleas and sucked again. His fingers dug into her wrist and pinned her to the tree.

"Your Highness, please let me go! It's poison! Don't put it in your mouth, or else—"

"Shut up," he said, voice low. There was a dangerous glint as he glowered at her for the first time in his life. "This is one time I refuse to grant your request." His shapely lips were red with her blood. He dragged the back of his hand over his mouth and murmured in a husky voice, "I thought I told you I won't allow you to die."

"Hngh!"

He bit and sucked, bit and sucked. Numbness overtook her as the poison faded from her skin, accompanied by a strange sensation somewhere between heat and pain. But the feeling gave her no relief, for her heart was in chaos.

Why? I don't want you to do something so dangerous! Oh, this is just like...

Rishe wanted to cry but felt hopelessly dizzy. She was weakening, losing her grip.

Ah, it really is...

She slowly shut her eyes as the world swayed around her.

It's like when I die.

That familiar feeling stole away her consciousness, and she sank into a warm sea.

7th TIME LOOP
The Villainess Enjoys a Carefree Life
Married to Her Worst Enemy!

WHEN RISHE SLEPT, she dreamed of her past lives. This time, she relived memories of her sixth loop. Painful memories of her blood spilling and arms trembling. Of her heart hammering against her chest while tried to protect her charges. Of the last day of her life.

"Evacuate His Highness and his family, quickly!"

"Our light, our lord! Protect him with your life! Get them out or die trying!"

Clashing swords and battle cries rang out all around her. The fight was so fierce that sparks flew. Her comrades died one after another. And the one responsible for this desperate situation was the enemy commander.

Arnold Hein.

Rishe glared at the man and gripped her bloodstained sword. His dark, muddy blue gaze swung in her direction. Her instincts screamed at her to run. The blood of Rishe's nearest and dearest slickened his frighteningly handsome face. His expression did not change in the slightest, but his eyes emitted an emotionless bloodlust that pierced her. Even in this oppressive atmosphere, practically paralyzed and breathless with tension, Rishe couldn't expose her back to him.

That man killed His Majesty, the commander, and the captain. Even Joel died protecting me.

She sucked in a breath and tightened her sword grip. She didn't care if she was killed pathetically. Her only wish was for the prince and his family to escape.

"Haaah!"

In an attempt to delay him, Rishe slashed desperately. Her fellow knights attacked him in turn, but he mowed them down, their bodies piling up around him. Eventually, no one else was left alive, and Arnold Hein's blade pierced Rishe's heart too.

Rishe dreamed of that one moment at the end of her life. But as her consciousness faded at the very end, Arnold Hein whispered in her ear.

Oh... Her memories of the end were vague, but that one moment replayed vividly. *I remember what he said to me back then.*

Then the dream faded around her, and she forgot everything she saw in it. Someone stroked her cheek. The sensation traded places with her memory, pulling her up out of the dark.

***

A gentle hand stroked her cheek, rousing Rishe from her sleep. The caress was careful, as if checking for a fever. She didn't know whose hand it was, but the way it touched her was so comforting. As it pulled away, her eyes opened.

Rishe groggily peered up at Arnold in a dark room filled with the quiet of night.

"Prince Arnold..."

Arnold sat beside her bed. She'd called his name, but he didn't respond. His knitted brows did not diminish the handsomeness of his face. His hand had definitely stirred her. But if this was her room in the Grand Basilica, what was Arnold doing there?

It was then that she finally recalled what had happened to her.

"Your Highness, how are you feeling?" she rasped, and the crease in Arnold's brow deepened.

"The first thing you do after waking up is worry about me?"

"Well, I..." She tried to explain herself, but she was feverish and lethargic. Her body felt like it was burning up, hot and heavy everywhere. Arnold sighed and slid his arm under Rishe's back.

"Ugh..."

Although she tried to rise with his assistance, she could barely move on her own. He ended up doing most of the work getting her to sit up. With one arm still behind her, his free hand reached toward her bedside table. Rishe recognized the small open bottle sitting there. Arnold picked up the bottle and pressed its rim to her lips.

"We just got this back. Drink it."

Rishe squeezed her lips shut and covered her mouth.

Arnold's frown evolved into a scowl. "I told you to drink it."

"I can't. Please drink it yourself, Your Highness." She looked up into his blue eyes and pleaded with him fervently. "Your health is more important than mine."

His eyes took on a chilly hue. Arnold brought the bottle to his own lips and silently downed it.

Rishe sighed with honest relief. *Good. If he drinks that, he'll be all right.*

Arnold must have had one of the five antidotes sent back to them. Were the seamstresses all right, assuming they'd taken the other four? From what Rishe knew of their symptoms, they had been suffering from high fevers. She hoped they wouldn't have to endure any lasting effects.

Still groggy, she noticed that Arnold's throat hadn't moved at all. As her sluggish mind worked to comprehend why, Arnold grasped her jaw and turned her face toward him. Then his lips came down on hers.

"Mmgh?!" Rishe's lips were pried open and a sickly-sweet fluid poured into her mouth. Once she realized what he was doing, she tried to resist, but her arms were like lead.

No! Prince Arnold must take this antidote!

But Arnold wouldn't let her go. He pulled her close and tilted her head back to make her swallow. At that point, her reflexes joined the fight against her will. Rishe swallowed, feeling pitiful for even attempting to resist.

"Agh!"

Arnold only let her go after he ascertained that she'd swallowed.

Bewildered, Rishe gawked at him. "Why?" she croaked.

He wiped his mouth with the back of his hand, then swept his thumb across Rishe's lips. His touch was gentle, but his eyes smoldered with irritation. "In case you can't tell, I'm rather angry at the moment."

Rishe winced.

The prince pressed his forehead against Rishe's and glared at her from up close. "I'm not going to apologize for being a little rough with you. This time, I don't mind if you slap me."

She kept her mouth shut and reached a hand out to Arnold, but it wasn't to hit him. Suppressing the urge to cry, she touched his lips. As she traced them, Arnold's anger gave way to dubiousness.

"What is it?"

"What about *your* antidote, Your Highness?"

Even though she was genuinely distressed, Arnold looked taken aback. His surprise melted into a frown, and he told her, "I spat your blood out right away, and I haven't experienced any adverse effects. I don't need one."

"It's a deadly poison! You might be safe while the sleeping drug is taking effect, but once your body absorbs it, there's a chance you'll die!"

"The fact that you unmistakably received a dose of the poison is more important to me."

His fingers touched Rishe's bandaged neck. The wound was hardly more than a scrape, but her neatly tied bandages were almost needlessly thorough.

"I believe I told you not to do anything dangerous." His voice was quiet but full of emotion.

"I'm sorry." Rishe's actions had even endangered Arnold. A royal—not to mention the very heir to the throne—ingesting poison was a serious incident, one that could've affected the fate of an entire nation had the worst happened. Just the thought of something happening to Arnold made her want to shrink with fear.

After giving her a meaningful look, Arnold laid Rishe back down. "Are you in pain?"

"No." She still felt heavy and feverish, but she could move all her extremities, albeit poorly. And since she'd been forced to take the antidote, her suffering would not be prolonged.

Rishe flexed her left hand, and Arnold placed his over top of it. Her elevated temperature made his feel cooler than usual. His blue eyes reflected the glow from the bedside lamp. It reminded her of something she'd seen in one of her lives: fires above the water used to lure fish at night.

"You're alive." Arnold stated the obvious, but his voice was seeking confirmation.

It felt like he wouldn't believe her if she simply said it, so Rishe grasped his hand as she told him, "Yes." Arnold sighed. Prompted by the look on his face, Rishe asked without thinking, "Have you watched someone you love die before?"

He broke eye contact and Rishe knew she'd asked a foolish question. The man had experienced war. He'd been directly involved in death countless times. His reply, however, caught her off guard.

"The first time was when my father murdered my sister."

Rishe couldn't process Arnold's quiet words. She understood them logically, but she couldn't wrap her head around the meaning. *His father murdered his sister?*

Arnold studied the speechless Rishe and explained, "A girl born to one of the emperor's wives. Mere days after the child came into the world, her mother did what she could to protect her, but he snatched her out of his wife's arms and ran his sword through her."

"No!" She refused to let her mind form the image.

Whenever the emperor emerged victorious over another nation, the conquered royal family would present him with a bride.

Rishe cursed her trembling voice as she asked, "Why would he do that?"

"That man only allowed children who clearly inherited his blood to live. He killed them in front of his wives to punish them for birthing ones who didn't."

Killing infants was bad enough, but this only confused Rishe further. How in the world did the emperor judge the worthiness of a days-old baby?

Arnold guessed what she was thinking. "My father only wanted children who had his black hair and blue eyes." He gazed down at Rishe with the very blue eyes he'd described. "He let only those children survive."

Rishe grimaced, overwhelmed. It wasn't just Arnold—Theodore, who had a different mother, also had black hair and blue eyes. His four younger sisters must've looked the same, but she'd had no idea of the reason.

That's why His Highness hates his eye color? She couldn't help remembering the conversation they'd had on his balcony in the detached palace. When she said his eyes were beautiful, he told her they were the same color as his father's eyes and that he hated them so much, he'd considered gouging them out more than once. She'd chalked it up to his hatred for his father, but apparently that wasn't all there was to it.

"Blue eyes are harder for children to inherit," she recalled. Add the condition of black hair and there would be very few children who fit his requirements indeed.

"You're right."

"Then, the children your father *didn't* accept?"

"He killed them without exception before their mothers' eyes."

Rishe was stunned. *How could he do something so abhorrent?!*

In her life as an apothecary, she had helped deliver several babies. It was not a sure thing by any means for mother and child to make it through the process in good health. Pregnancy was a harrowing nine-month experience. Mothers bore pain and anxiety and risked their lives to birth children. And just like that, their father had snuffed out those young lives?

"He made you watch when you were still young?"

His silent affirmation made her chest tighten even more.

"Was anyone there for you? The emperor's wives, they..."

"They resented me for surviving and had nothing but hatred in their hearts for me." His next words were so quiet, it was as if he was only talking to himself. "My own mother hated me the most."

A strangled sound escaped her throat, and Arnold linked his fingers with hers. His voice was calm and composed as he continued, "When he killed them, he would say to me, 'The blood that flows through your veins is superior to everyone else's.'" His slender fingers traced the ring Rishe wore. "But that's not true. What value could there possibly be in that man's bloodline?"

"Oh, Your Highness..."

"I want you to understand this too. Even if I'm royalty, no matter whose blood I inherit, that doesn't make me any more important than anyone else," Arnold said sincerely. "Never say that my life is more important than yours again."

Rishe's heart thumped hard. "I..." She wanted to say, *I can't do that,* but the words wouldn't come. She met his eyes and slowly, carefully blinked.

The next moment, the tears she'd been holding back spilled forth.

"Hey," Arnold said, alarmed, pulling his hand out of hers. He touched her bandages and scanned her in dismay. It was rare to see such consternation on his face. "I knew it. You *are* in pain."

"No, I'm not!" She tried to deny it, but her voice shook treacherously. She pressed her hands to her eyelids, but the tears kept falling.

As she wept uncontrollably, Arnold asked, perplexed, "Why are you crying?"

"I-I'm sorry!" Rishe had her own complaints about Arnold's circumstances, but her attempts to hide her distress weren't working. She couldn't even remember the last time she'd cried in front of someone. "You're just so kind."

That only compounded his bewilderment.

Rishe had noticed that some knights who returned from dangerous battlefields fought with no regard for their lives. When asked why they did so, they replied that it was their punishment for surviving. They felt guilty that their comrades died but they survived, so in repentance, they went out to more battlefields. But surviving wasn't a sin.

"You didn't do anything wrong when you were a child, and yet..."

Arnold was *acting* like he had. During the bandit attack, when he dismissed his knights to fight them off with his own sword. The battle in Ceutena that Fritz had described. Even when Rishe herself faced him in her sixth life. In all those cases, he stood on the front lines of battle himself to atone for the sins he felt he'd committed.

I'm sure he's been doing this since he was very young.

The thought squeezed heat and fresh tears from Rishe's eyes. Her heart ached. Arnold finally seemed to understand that she wasn't crying from physical pain.

"Don't rub your eyes so much."

"Hngh..."

He grabbed her arms. Her vision unobscured, she saw his blurry features. Each time she blinked, the world focused a little more but quickly blurred again. She could just barely make out the stumped look on Arnold's face.

"Come now." One of his hands wiped away her tears. Still frowning, he asked, "What'll it take for you to stop crying?"

Even *more* tears rolled down her cheeks.

"Rishe."

"Well..." Rishe began. He was only concerned for her and thought nothing of his own suffering. Her powerlessness was only exacerbated by her paralyzing fever. All that compounded into a wish even she didn't understand as it issued from her mouth.

"Y-your hair..."

"My head?"

"I want to...stroke your hair, Prince Arnold," she told him. The furrow in Arnold's brow deepened.

"Listen to yourself."

She was aware it was an absurd thing to ask of a nineteen-year-old man. Nevertheless, she wanted to stroke his hair—to comfort him—more than anything. She knew she couldn't reach the child Arnold, so she wanted to do it for the Arnold of the present. With an imploring gaze, she pressed, "Please, Your Highness."

Arnold sighed deeply and climbed into the bed. The springs creaked and the sheets rustled. He cupped Rishe's face and leaned over her; this way, he was close enough to touch. In a throaty voice, he acquiesced to her request. "Do what you want."

"Th-thank you." Still weeping, Rishe reached up and caressed Arnold's head. It was a peculiar sensation. Arnold wasn't used to this, and Rishe wasn't doing a good job. Still, she gently and rhythmically stroked his black hair. Arnold's hair, which ended in slight curls, was softer to the touch than she expected. Even this overwhelmed Rishe, eliciting more sobs.

"Hey." Arnold made a face like she'd pulled a fast one on him. She knew she was causing him further consternation, but she couldn't help herself. "Rishe..."

"I'm...I'm so sorry..."

"Damn it."

Arnold touched his forehead to hers. There was a rustling sound as his hair brushed against hers. He closed his eyes.

"Please, don't cry anymore," he begged her, voice laced with pain. "I can't handle seeing you cry."

"Ngh..."

He was beside himself because she wouldn't stop crying, but she couldn't keep from bawling like a child. It was hard for her to see him suffering too. Rishe had been forbidden to cry in front of her parents, so this was a new experience.

Arnold was completely at a loss the whole time, but he continued wiping away Rishe's tears until she cried herself to sleep.

***

"Mmh..."

Rishe awoke feeling light and warm. She felt like she'd dreamed of her time in Galkhein while she slept—of her conversation with Arnold on his balcony at the detached palace, of a party they'd attended, dreams of things that had occurred mere days ago. It was the first time in a long while that Rishe dreamed of something other than her past lives.

She yearned to stay in bed and nestled up to whatever lay

next to her. Although she didn't know what it was, she felt she fit in it perfectly, warmly wrapped around her as it was. It emitted a comforting sound similar to a heartbeat.

"Hm?"

Her eyelids were heavy and so was the rest of her body, but the sluggishness from the night before was gone. It seemed she would suffer no lasting effects from the poison. So why the odd feeling of extra weight? She squirmed and slowly opened her eyes—and finally understood.

Arnold was asleep in her bed, his arms wrapped around her. Rishe felt a screech coming on, but she managed to stifle it somehow.

Wh-wh-wha—?!

They had apparently fallen asleep facing each other, curled up under the same bedspread. Arnold snored softly as he held Rishe's head to his chest. His lips were buried in her hair.

Wh-why am I in the same bed as His Highness?!

She realized with some panic that Arnold was the only one using the pillow; she had co-opted his arm. Yet she was entirely too frazzled to do anything about it. Then she remembered how all of this transpired in the first place.

This is because of the tantrum I threw!

Rishe's face drained of all color as she remembered the night before.

I asked him to return to his room to get some sleep, but he said, "I can't just leave you alone. I'll stay with you through the night." And then I went and said, "If you insist on staying in this room, then don't stay up all night. At least sleep here..."

She fried her brain crying her eyes out, so she'd said something completely outrageous. Arnold had shot her a look of utter shock, but since she almost started crying again, he'd ended up reluctantly agreeing to stay the night. She couldn't believe what she'd done. She felt miserable for making Arnold stay with her the whole time.

How could a proud apothecary do such a thing?! I should have made him go back to his room and rest properly by himself!

Rishe gently pulled away from Arnold and regarded him with worry.

I hope he didn't sleep poorly with me in his arms.

Though she was sure that Arnold would have awoken as soon as Rishe stirred, he still slept. She didn't know if he was tired from looking after her or if he really was affected by the poison, but she hoped he was recovering. So she prayed as she watched him sleep.

He looks younger when he sleeps.

The top two buttons of Arnold's white shirt were undone. In this relaxed state of dress, his collarbones and Adam's apple, usually hidden, were visible. Rishe's eyes were drawn to the countless scars at the base of his neck.

Arnold said his mother hated him the most. Did she give him these scars?

Much as she wanted to touch them, it would have been rude to do so without his permission, so she just stared at them in a daze. Arnold's hand began to twitch as if in search of something.

His eyelids fluttered open, revealing half-awake blue eyes lit by the morning sunlight streaming through the window.

Normally, Rishe would be captivated by them, but there was no time for that at the moment.

"Erm, good morning," she said.

Arnold blinked sluggishly and brushed Rishe's coral hair from her eyes. He put his hand on her cheek and closed his eyes while touching his forehead to hers. He must have been checking for a fever. Rishe knew that, but she couldn't help her nervousness.

"Your Highness, I—"

"How are you feeling?" he asked, voice thick with sleep.

With their foreheads still touching, their eyelashes nearly brushed against each other. "I-I'm fine," Rishe stammered. "Thanks to you, Your Highness, I'm c-completely recovered!"

Arnold frowned, eyes fully open now. Well, "completely" was probably a stretch, Rishe reflected. Feeling awkward, she tried to sit up, but Arnold grabbed her arm.

"Eep!"

"Just keep resting."

She sank down into the sea of the bed, drawn back into Arnold's arms. She felt she couldn't stay there, but she didn't think she was in a position to argue. Having no other choice, Rishe relaxed and asked, "How are *you* feeling, Your Highness?"

"Fine," Arnold said, touching Rishe's neck. He was undoing her bandages.

Rishe lay still and let him work. "Thank you for everything you did yesterday. Um, is Lady Millia all right?"

"I had Oliver tell the duke that someone was targeting her."

Relief washed over her. She knew Arnold wouldn't let her down, but it was still good to hear.

"I told the girl to stay by her father's side too. Oliver reported to me in the middle of the night that she was behaving herself and staying with the duke."

"Did Lady Millia tell you where I was?"

"Yeah. Leo told me what happened, and I ran into her on my way to the forest."

There was the quiet rustle of cloth as Arnold unwrapped her bandages. He explained everything she'd been wanting to ask him, but she wished they weren't facing each other in bed while he did it.

"I told Leo and the girl to keep quiet about being in the forest. It'll just cause needless commotion if the Church finds out."

"You really thought of everything. Truly, thank y—ah!" Rishe flinched when Arnold's fingers touched her skin directly.

"Stay still."

"But that tickles! Hee hee hee! Wait!"

"I told you to stay still," Arnold chided her.

She did her best to endure the discomfort until she was finally freed from her wrappings. Then it occurred to her that she could have just taken them off herself. However, Arnold was now examining her wound with thoroughness, so she couldn't bring herself to point that out.

"Looks like your wound is healing. Doesn't look like it'll leave a scar."

That didn't matter to Rishe. In her sixth loop, she was covered in scars. She said nothing as she reached up to feel the spot for herself.

Arnold stared into her eyes next. "Looks like your eyes aren't swollen, either."

"Well, you wiped my tears away so carefully, Prince Arnold," Rishe said with some embarrassment.

At last, he seemed satisfied. "Let me wrap it back up. I'll get some fresh bandages."

"Oh, it's fine." Arnold sat up, so Rishe sat up with him. "The bleeding's stopped, so it'll be fine to just leave it like this. It wasn't a bad cut, so I think it's a bit silly to bandage it."

"I think you should bandage it."

"Huh?"

"It's red. It's probably best to hide it."

Rishe tilted her head to one side, puzzled. "I didn't think this poison caused inflammation at the site of the wound."

He didn't answer her. This poison was chosen for assassinations precisely because it left no identifiable traces. Or was there something Rishe hadn't anticipated mixed in with the poison? If she was wrong about the poison, though, the antidote shouldn't have worked as well as it did. Thanks to the antidote her master had taught her to make, and Arnold forcing her to take it, Rishe was nearly fully recovered.

Arnold pulled her from her musings. "I'm not talking about the wound."

"Hmm?"

His fingers traced her skin, and Rishe hunched her shoulders at the ticklish sensation. It wasn't the wound Arnold had touched but the skin around it.

He explained nonchalantly, "It turned red where I sucked on it."

Rishe's mouth fell open. Had he just said something completely outrageous? He must have been talking about when he sucked the poison, but her mind flitted to the things Arnold did to her the night before all over again.

"It stands out all the more because your skin is so pale."

"Eep?!" A belated heat rose to her cheeks. She snatched the covers up to hide what she could only assume was her bright-red face. She didn't even want to see Arnold's expression right now.

Wait, when he gave me the antidote yesterday, didn't he also do it mouth-to-mouth?!

Her body felt hotter now than when she had a fever.

As her head spun, Rishe managed to squeak out, "There's, um, something I've been wondering about you, Your Highness!"

"What is it?"

Wait, I can't ask him why he acts so familiar with women!

Or was this normal? She wanted to ask, but she was too afraid and didn't know where that feeling was coming from.

"Rishe," Arnold said while her emotions spiraled. "Why did you entrust Leo with your message for me?"

That stopped Rishe's emotional whirlwind in its tracks. Slowly, she peeked over the top of the blankets. "I thought I had to find Lady Millia as soon as possible because I feared the worst."

"That's not what I meant." When their eyes met, Arnold was expressionless—but he wasn't going to let Rishe get out of this one, it seemed. He'd gotten plenty mad at her last night and wasn't showing her any mercy. "You can't tell me you really think he's trustworthy."

His cold gaze pierced Rishe, as if the mood between them up until now had been an illusion. She took a breath. It was true; she couldn't attribute her suspicions about the way Leo moved to just over-training.

I'm not surprised Prince Arnold noticed too.

The day before yesterday, in the forest, Rishe had walked with a fixed stride. Doing that had allowed her to create a mental map of the path she'd taken. This was useful in unfamiliar places, and that information had helped her find Millia the next day. What was unnatural was how Leo had acted while Rishe was measuring her steps.

Back then, Leo matched my pace perfectly.

He had walked neither faster nor slower. His pace had been in sync with hers in the forest in spite of the unstable footing. That meant that Leo was either measuring his steps as well or he was purposely matching her pace.

"Odd of him to know about body doubles for royalty as well," Arnold said.

Rishe felt the same way. It might have made sense if Leo had been more involved with royals or nobles, but if the practice was known among the common people, it wouldn't have any meaning. His imagination running wild would be one thing, but Leo had specifically said he'd *heard* it before. There were just too many peculiarities about him to convincingly call him a "normal kid."

"You had your doubts about him too. That's why you didn't mention the antidote when you sent him to me with a message."

"I was pressed for time, mostly. I believed you'd know exactly what I wanted you to do, Prince Arnold."

"I can't imagine you went out of your way to gamble in a situation like that. It wasn't just your own safety on the line but that of the priestess girl too." Arnold sat on the edge of the bed. "I had Oliver investigate the carriage's broken axle some more. They hired several drivers to throw off the scent, but it was the Church who originally prepared the carriage."

Rishe squeezed the sheets in her hands. "Then..."

"The ones who are trying to kill the new priestess are from the very Church tasked with protecting her."

She already knew, but hearing the words still produced a sick ache in her chest. A forbidden forest without even a lookout, their policy of letting in as few servants and guards as possible... Since it was the Church's scheme, the goddess's teachings and the festival were just excuses.

The Church that's supposed to protect her is trying to kill Mistress Millia, the genuine royal priestess.

When Rishe lapsed into silence, Arnold said, "Leo was walking to make noise on purpose."

Her eyes widened; she hadn't expected that. "Do you mean to say that Leo would make no sound at all if he walked normally?"

"That's right. But that would make him stand out, so he goes out of his way to do so."

It is *rather easy to pick out Leo's footsteps.*

They naturally sounded different than those of adults, but there was also a clear difference between his and Millia's footsteps despite their similar weights. Rishe had just assumed that she could tell them apart because she knew them from her previous lives.

Prince Arnold picked up on that just from watching Leo walk?

His observations had surpassed Rishe's in a matter of minutes. She was surprised yesterday, but she was utterly shocked today.

"I don't need to tell you why someone would teach a child a skill like that."

"I almost wish you did."

"Well, regardless of your *wishes*, when you put the facts together, everything becomes clear." Arnold paused, then stated the brutal truth: "Leo has been trained as an assassin."

Rishe nodded, eyes downcast. The reason for the peculiar way he moved and the excessive training he'd gone through at his age was because he'd grown up in a very particular environment. She and Arnold agreed on this point.

"If you knew that, why'd you send him with the message?"

"Well, you agreed to teach him despite your suspicions, Your Highness. Isn't that because you hadn't yet determined where his allegiances lie?"

Arnold's brow scrunched ever so slightly. "It was nothing so dramatic. I just thought if I brought him back and gave him to Theodore, my brother would find some way to make use of him."

That was a lie. Arnold had agreed to teach Leo even after he said he wouldn't go back to Galkhein with them.

"In all likelihood, Leo was trained to be an assassin at Bishop Schneider's orphanage. He would only have left the orphanage if there was no reason to keep him anymore. Either he was acknowledged as an assassin and sent to work, or he was deemed a failure and released."

"What, you think Leo's already washed his hands off the assassination business?"

"No, Prince Arnold." Rishe met Arnold's eyes. "I believe that Leo *is* an assassin."

Arnold took a quiet breath. "Then why send him to me?"

"Because I judged that he wasn't a threat even if he is an assassin. I believe he's too kind to make a career out of killing people."

On the day they arrived at the Grand Basilica, Leo had ridden his horse as fast as he could to inform them that the duke's carriage had crashed. When Millia went missing, Leo explained the situation to Rishe with a genuinely pale face. If he were trying to kill Millia, all he had to do was keep quiet and then tell a convincing lie later. Yet he'd gone so far as to seek Arnold for his help.

"I took advantage of that fact. I judged that, no matter Leo's skills, he was too kind to take a person's life."

That was why she'd forced Leo and Millia to interact with each other even though she knew it was cruel. After all, Rishe knew his future. Leo was destined to screw up at his job and lose his eye to a beating from his employer.

His injuries were so bad that if he hadn't escaped, I'm sure he would have been killed.

That "employer" wasn't Millia's father, the duke. It was the person he worked for as an assassin.

His "mistake" might have been made during his attempt to assassinate Mistress Millia. Perhaps Duke Jonal's paralysis by way of illness was a lie, and it was actually inflicted by a poisoning he received in Mistress Millia's place.

Though Rishe and the seamstresses had survived their poisoning, if their treatment had come too late, they could have been paralyzed in much the same way. Now that she thought back on it, Duke Jonal's symptoms could absolutely have been caused by this poison compound.

His Grace probably lied about it in my fourth loop.

Duke Jonal hadn't wanted to tell the truth of his condition for Millia's sake. He might have changed out all his servants for fear of one of them telling her the truth.

The duke's paralysis and Leo's terrible injuries must both come back to the events here at the Grand Basilica.

All the chaos had probably been the cause of the clergymen's dismissals. Millia blamed herself for the misfortunes and brought that wound with her all the way to adulthood.

I need to make sure that Leo never carries out the assassination, and that the duke and Mistress Millia go home safely. But if the enemy targeting Mistress Millia is the most powerful Church in the world, what can I do?

It became too much for her to bear, and she murmured, "Why would the Church want to kill the royal priestess?"

Arnold gave a small snort. Her head shot up in surprise.

"Do you really believe the Church wants to *protect* the royal priestess?" he asked.

What is he saying? She couldn't ask him because she'd caught on to the same thing. "You're referring to the death of the previous royal priestess twenty-two years ago."

"Heh. What do you think?" He chuckled as if he found it funny, but there was a darkness in his smile. Rishe had seen that smile somewhere before.

The previous priestess would have died a few years before Prince Arnold was born.

He couldn't have been personally familiar with the accident, but something about this just didn't sit right with Rishe.

I've been wondering about this since my fourth loop.

If they really wanted to protect Millia, why not announce her status officially and protect her with the full force of their organization? The royal priestess was the reincarnation of the goddess, an object of worship for the faithful worldwide. If her existence was publicized, surely it would be easier to guarantee her safety. So why had they hidden her existence and had a duke adopt her?

"Rishe." Arnold smiled and met her gaze. "Do you want to save that priestess girl?"

Rishe nodded firmly.

Arnold's large hand stroked her cheek and tilted her head up. "The festival will proceed today as scheduled," he said softly. "They rushed the preparations so that everything could go as planned."

"Oh no!"

The archbishop, the other bishops, and royal priestess Millia were the festival's central figures. She would be alone with the very group of people trying to kill her. Whatever happened there, no one would protect her.

"Why would they agree to that after you warned them about the assassination? The duke couldn't possibly have ruled out the Church as suspect."

"That's a strange thing to say."

Rishe gave Arnold a confused look.

"Duke Jonal is a devout believer. He's raising the priestess precisely because the Church ordered him to, is he not?"

"Huh?"

"Now the Church wishes for her death. In this situation, what reason would the duke have to protect a child he didn't father?"

Arnold honestly believed his words. Rishe hurried to refute him. "That's not true! Lady Millia is Duke Jonal's precious daughter. He would never expose her to danger no matter what the Church wishes, regardless of any blood ties."

She knew full well how the duke cherished Millia and how much care he took in raising her. His love for her was real; it surpassed any blood ties or orders from the Church.

"I want to save them. Lady Millia and Leo and Duke Jonal—all of them!"

Arnold's gaze dropped. "Then don't worry." His next words to her were gentle. "If that's what you want, I'll make it happen."

"Are you sure, Your Highness?"

Arnold stood from the bed and picked up his jacket from a nearby chair, then shrugged it on. "You keep resting for a little longer," he told her, leaving the room and closing the door quietly behind him.

I have Prince Arnold on my side. Nothing should be more reassuring, but...

Worry still lapped at her heart like waves. Rishe stood, her mouth taut in a hard line, and began to get ready.

7th TIME LOOP
The Villainess Enjoys a Carefree Life
Married to Her Worst Enemy!

CHAPTER 6

MUCH OF THE GRAND BASILICA was deserted. Rishe's footsteps reverberated off the silent halls. Now dressed, Rishe peeked into the cathedral hall nearest the guest building and found it just as empty. Up until yesterday, the place had been packed with bishops offering prayers to the goddess and monks busy with festival preparations.

There's no one here. It's not just Mistress Millia and Duke Jonal...I don't see Prince Arnold or Oliver anywhere either.

Had they all headed for the cathedral? Regular worshippers were forbidden from attending the festival rite. Not even Arnold was permitted inside the cathedral right now.

Why am I so uneasy? Rishe's mouth was a tight frown as she ran toward the cathedral. *In the future, Emperor Arnold Hein burns churches and priests. Right now, Prince Arnold shouldn't take such drastic actions...but why did he order the Church personnel to stay away from me?*

There had to be a reason for his future enmity. In her past lives, Rishe assumed he'd gone after the Church simply because it was a nuisance. People all over the world relied on the Church's authority. It was nothing but an eyesore for someone who wished to rule over those people, and he had no reason to permit its existence.

Still, I'm sure that's only one of his reasons.

In the distance, a bell rang, signifying the beginning of the festival. Rishe lifted her skirt to dash faster, but a moment later...

"Ah! Leo!"

A boy jumped out in front of her and Rishe skidded to a stop. Leo stood and looked her in the eyes.

She gulped. *I really didn't hear a thing. I didn't sense him coming at all!*

Observing her, Leo cautiously asked, "You're going to the cathedral?"

"Yes. The festival's about to start, isn't it?"

Leo scowled. "If not for the urgent meeting Arnold Hein just called with the archbishop."

"Prince Arnold? I can't imagine the archbishop agreeing to such a thing right before the festival."

"I'm sure he used their treaty. I hear the Church can't refuse when Galkhein requests a meeting with them."

Rishe's eyes widened. *I didn't know Galkhein and the Church had a treaty.*

The boy snorted when he saw her reaction. "You had no idea."

Even if they do have a treaty like that, there's no way they'd prioritize it over the festival. The meeting isn't Prince Arnold's motive, then.

Rishe grimaced.

It's making the Church break *their treaty.*

She was certain of it.

I don't know the consequences for breaking the treaty, but it's possible that Prince Arnold will use that as an excuse to intrude upon the festival.

A chill crept down Rishe's back. Even if she couldn't trust in Emperor Arnold Hein, she'd assumed the nineteen-year-old Arnold she knew wouldn't needlessly antagonize the Church. Maybe that assumption was wrong. Galkhein and the Church had some sort of agreement. If the Church broke their end of the agreement, it would be easy for Arnold to act against them. He must've asked for a meeting he didn't even want because he was looking to position himself at the ready.

Prince Arnold has the perfect justification for his actions as long as he's saving Mistress Millia.

Arnold would actually gain the support of believers worldwide if his mission was to protect the royal priestess from the Church.

He's such a kind man. That's why he's able to go to extreme lengths to protect someone.

Rishe was certain he would try to rescue Millia to fulfill her wish...by any means necessary.

"I have to go."

She had to save Millia, but she also had to prevent Arnold from doing anything too drastic. Much as she didn't want to believe she'd been mistaken to ask for his help, she also found herself cursing her hastiness.

Rishe tried to hasten on, but Leo's small body blocked her path. "I can't let you get any closer to the cathedral."

"Leo."

"I can't take my eyes off you for a second, so I have no choice but to give you a warning. If you're allied with Arnold Hein, then I can't let you go."

Overcome with sadness, Rishe clenched her fists. "I can't be Prince Arnold's ally."

Leo blinked, wide-eyed.

"Thank you for worrying about me, Leo...but I'm sorry." Rishe looked right at him and told him, "There are things that I have to do at his side even if it means becoming his enemy."

"I warned you!"

Rishe made to run, so Leo leaped in her way to cut her off. He tried to grab her wrist, so she swiftly dodged. She stepped back, putting distance between herself and Leo, and tried to steady her breathing.

Leo immediately closed the gap.

He's fast!

She didn't even have the time to let her surprise show. Leo's hand shot toward her collar. The moment he touched her dress, she whirled out of his reach. He reached for her again, so she lightly struck his wrist.

Hand knocked away, Leo sprang back. "You really are a lousy body double. The way you move, it's completely obvious you're not the real princess."

"And I suppose you don't need to play the part of the normal boy anymore, do you?"

"There's no point with you two. Not with you watching my every move and pointing out everything I'm trying to hide!"

He charged her, but Rishe dodged at the last second. Leo kept up his attack, going for Rishe's wrist, then trying to sweep her legs when she avoided him. Rishe was playing keep-away, but every time she dodged, he got right back up next to her.

Ugh! I don't even have time to breathe!

Now that she thought about it, she'd always been up against bigger opponents. She barely had any experience fighting someone smaller, like Leo. It was throwing her off and putting her at a distinct disadvantage.

He's so quick! If I let my attention waver for a moment, he'll get me!

Leo reached for her again. She avoided him, struck at him, tried to pull away. The moment she considered running past him, he closed in on her once more. Leo's arms, slender and flexible, sped to capture her.

I'm not used to fighting like this, so...

Rishe took a breath and then reached out to Leo herself. She gripped his wrist and tugged it backward. When he lost his balance, she swooped in behind him, grabbed his clothes, and pulled him toward her. Leo clicked his tongue and tried to get low to the ground, but Rishe was anticipating it.

This is my only way out!

"Agh!"

Rishe used Leo's movement to pull him to the ground herself. He tried to regain his balance, but Rishe swept his legs out from under him and threw him down.

"Damn it!"

If he has one, he'll use a weapon here!

While on his back, Leo threw something he had hidden in his sleeve at Rishe. She dodged it on reflex and realized it was a small stone. Rishe flipped Leo over and reached for her skirt's hem. She bound his hands behind him with the rope she kept fixed to her thigh.

"Let me go!"

Ignoring his cries, she looped the rope around his wrists and tied it with a difficult knot. She didn't plan on keeping him tied up for too long, so she didn't need to break his bones.

"I can't believe this! You know all my moves?!"

"Of course I do. I'm well versed in how to fight with a small build."

Leo's technique was top-class, but that made him easy to read. He wasted no movements and aimed with complete precision, so Rishe could anticipate his moves exactly.

"Long-range weapons lack stopping power: stones, throwing knives, and even arrows." Rishe stood and dusted her dress. "They're challenging to use, and they're not very lethal. It's so hard to kill with them, in fact, that you must coat them in poison to be sure you take your target out."

"So what?"

"You have the poison on you, don't you?"

Leo's strawberry-red eyes glared up at Rishe.

"If you'd used it just now, you might have been able to stop me. So why didn't you?"

"Very funny coming from someone who didn't give me a single chance to hit her," Leo said bitterly, but he was lying. After all, Rishe was rapidly losing stamina. Although she feigned composure, her bandages were soaked with sweat.

I'm so exhausted. I feel faint and dizzy, like I'm anemic... Our skirmish was awful on my body. My stamina's so drained from the poison.

Rishe wanted to head for the cathedral as soon as possible, but she couldn't run until she caught her breath. She trained every morning but found it difficult to build stamina. Concealing her belabored breathing, she looked down at Leo.

"You didn't use a poisoned weapon because you were worried about me, right?"

"No."

"Oh no, I think I'm right. You're a sweet kid; you're not suited to killing people."

"Stop it! Stop talking like my family or sister or something when you've only known me for a few days!" From the ground, Leo glared at Rishe. "I needed to stop you. Even if I died here or had to kill you."

"Oh, Leo..."

"Why?!" Leo's small shoulders shook, causing her to gasp.

It couldn't be!

Kneeling before him, she sat him up and looked into his eyes. "Leo."

He said nothing.

"Who is your enemy?"

All this time, she'd been wrong. What she asked him now, she asked to determine if her hunch was correct.

Leo seemed to be enduring something for a moment, and then he drooped, resigned, and sighed as if he were much older. "My enemy is Galkhein." Leo looked up into Rishe's eyes. "And the bishops of the Crusade."

She'd been wrong about Leo—wrong about why he'd learned to fight, why he'd been hastily taken under the duke's employ, and why he'd accompanied them to the festival as well.

Leo's not here to kill Mistress Millia. He's here to protect her!

In her sixth loop, Leo had made a mistake at his former job. Rishe had assumed that mistake was failing an assassination, but if Leo was a guard and not an assassin, then his mistake would have been failing to protect Millia and her father. That was why Leo had always seemed angry about something in that life. What if he had been angry at himself for failing in his mission and letting the duke get hurt?

That's why he wanted Prince Arnold to train him so he could become stronger. It wasn't so that he could kill better, but so he could protect someone better.

Rishe's fists tightened as she masked her alarm. "Are you Lady Millia's guard?"

"Not after how badly I screwed up. I took my eyes off her, put her in danger, and on top of that, *you* were the one who saved her."

"You said the bishops of the Crusade were your enemies. Does that mean it's the archbishop and Bishop Schneider who are after Lady Millia's life?"

Leo didn't answer, averting his eyes. But there was something else he'd said that she couldn't ignore.

"Why do you say Galkhein's your enemy?"

"Because the Church..." Leo took a short breath. "At this rate, Galkhein will wipe us out."

Rishe's breath caught. He spoke as if he knew the future.

Does that mean the Church already knows why Prince Arnold will attack them?

That cleared up one of her remaining questions. Arnold had warned the duke that Millia was being targeted, yet the duke had handed her over to the Church for the festival without suspicion. It wasn't that he didn't believe Arnold's warning.

It was the opposite. He perceived it as a threat!

If the very person who had a reason to kill his beloved daughter told him that she was in danger, the father would be on his guard and rush to finish their business as soon as possible so that they could leave.

If Prince Arnold had predicted even that last night, then he was speeding the festival along so that he could pick a fight with the Church as soon as possible!

But what reason did Arnold have to go to such lengths? The more she thought about it, the more confused she became. What was most important now was that she had to hurry.

"I'm sorry, Leo."

"Are you sure you just wanna leave me here tied up? It'll take a while, but I can get out of it."

"That's fine. I'm not your enemy." She was breathing a lot easier now. With just a bit more time, she would be able to move again no matter how incomplete her recovery had been. "I want to protect Lady Millia. And I want to prevent Prince Arnold from clashing with the Church too. As such, our interests align."

Leo frowned and muttered, "Are you serious? Are you really Galkhein's crown princess?"

"Not until I can annul my engagement ceremony properly. I can't do that if we start a fight with the Church."

"..."

"You know, Leo." Rishe smiled, remembering her sixth loop. In that life, Leo had always looked angry. He never interacted with people as he watched their training from afar, and Rishe hadn't been able to leave him alone. She'd taken every opportunity to talk to him, even though he drove her away as if she annoyed him each time. She did that for almost five years, so she couldn't help acting like a concerned sister, just as he'd said. "There was a boy a lot like you whom I always thought of as a little brother. So when you told me not to talk like your sister earlier, it made me a little happy."

"Wha...?"

"If we can, I'd like to talk to you some more later," Rishe told him before she left.

"The Goddess Tower!" Leo called out to her as she walked away.

She wheeled around in surprise.

Leo lowered his head and told her, "The archbishop and Millia aren't in the cathedral."

"What?"

"The cathedral is for large events with big crowds, but real holy ceremonies take place at the Goddess Tower in the innermost part of the Grand Basilica."

Rishe recalled the mental map of the Grand Basilica from her fourth loop. In the future she knew, there was no such place as the "Goddess Tower," but there *was* a tower deep in the Grand Basilica that was off-limits.

"Thank you, Leo."

"You believe me? What if I'm lying?"

"It's all right." Rishe grinned. Rather than the ladylike smile of a noblewoman, it was the boyish smirk she would've worn in her life as a knight. "If you truly lied to me, I bet you'll shout 'Wait, I lied!' before I'm out of earshot."

"Oh, shut up!"

Rishe apologized, somewhat flustered by his outburst, and took off for the Goddess Tower.

"What a strange lady," Leo muttered to himself, left alone in the hall. The knot around his wrists was awfully complex. He didn't think it'd be completely impossible to get out of, but it *would* take considerable effort. "Damn it! If she's really not in the same business, then what *is* she?"

After clicking his tongue, Leo looked off in the direction that Rishe had gone. "The future empress of Galkhein, huh?"

***

Rishe ran to the innermost area of the Grand Basilica, taking care not to get dizzy. Leo's revelation was whirling in her head.

Leo said Galkhein was one of his enemies. He didn't mention Prince Arnold but named the country itself. Why?

The full picture was getting clearer, but some core pieces of the puzzle were still missing. It was causing her no small amount of anxiety.

I'm guessing the duke pulled me away from Mistress Millia because he didn't want me realizing she was the royal priestess.

Still, it felt a little unnatural.

It's like he specifically didn't want me *to find out.*

The events of the day before yesterday came to mind.

When I first met Mistress Millia in this life, Prince Arnold gave her the coldest glare. The duke also grew nervous the moment Prince Arnold named himself.

Was there anything else that had struck her as strange?

Something I heard here at the Grand Basilica... Something about Prince Arnold, about his childhood.

One possibility emerged in Rishe's mind.

No way!

She could hardly believe what she was thinking as she finally arrived at the tower and barged through the doors. The chamber inside was the size of a chapel. There was an entrance hall just inside the doors with twin staircases to the left and right. Rishe ascended one of them and spotted someone else when she got to the third floor.

"Oliver!"

"Oh, Lady Rishe." Oliver turned around casually, but Schneider was lying at his feet. The bishop appeared to be unconscious, blood dripping from the corner of his mouth. Rishe was startled, but he didn't seem seriously injured. It looked like he'd just been taken out with a single well-placed hit. "Well, this isn't good. I could have sworn I sent a monk with a message telling you to rest in your room, Lady Rishe."

"Was this Prince Arnold's doing?"

"Yes. My lord is a few floors higher, pursuing the archbishop." Oliver pointed upward with a smile.

She swallowed hard. Oliver never batted an eyelash at anything Arnold did, but seeing him like this admittedly scared her a bit. "I'm going after him."

"I wouldn't if I were you. My lord is in a rather foul mood. You *were* injured, after all."

Rishe blinked, surprised. She got the feeling that Oliver had donned a liar's smile, however. "Thank you for the warning! But if Prince Arnold isn't thinking clearly, then that's all the more reason someone has to stop him!"

She headed upstairs, shoulders heaving, out of breath again even though she'd just rested. When she had nearly reached the sixth floor, she finally noticed something out of place: an arrow lying on one of the steps.

This is one of the sacred tools used in the festival!

Plucking it from the step, she looked up and saw several more arrows scattered on the stairs. She bit her lip when she saw the accompanying bow.

Mistress Millia reveres the goddess. She would never leave the sacred tools on the ground if she dropped them. Either she wasn't in a situation where she could pick them up, or she wasn't in any condition to—

Scooping up the bow and arrows, Rishe ran until she reached the seventh floor.

"Prince Arnold!"

Arnold slowly turned to face her, his sword drawn. Instinctively, Rishe shuddered in fear. The man in front of her was the very picture of the emperor who had slain her in her sixth loop. Unlike then, the monks lying around were still breathing, and the look in Arnold's eyes as he stared at her lacked that too-familiar icy bloodlust.

"What is it, Rishe?" Arnold reached out to her, gaze strangely gentle. "You're out of breath—and so pale."

"Your Highness, you..."

"I'm sure you pushed yourself to get here, didn't you?" He stroked her cheek, his hand reeking of blood. "I'll save the priestess girl. You don't need to worry about anything."

Rishe flinched.

"Just be good and wait." He spoke coaxingly, but his tone brooked no argument. "You can do that, can't you?" Arnold fixed his sea-colored eyes on Rishe. The light in them was dark and sharp like a blade.

"There's something I'd like to ask you first."

Why had Arnold wanted the people of the Church to stay away from Rishe? She remembered the day they arrived at the Grand Basilica. Rishe and Arnold had talked on the balcony, but before that, Rishe had spoken to Bishop Schneider.

"That's why only a woman born to the priestess's bloodline can be chosen for the position."

"There are a few men in the family, so the goddess's precious bloodline has not died out completely."

"The late royal priestess was highly proficient. I doubt we'll ever see someone of her fluency again."

Rishe inhaled deeply. Millia was her mother's only child. After her mother died, Millia became the only female descendant of the royal priestess. That was why she was raised in secret.

But what if there was another woman whose existence was hidden?

Just like the Church concealed Millia.

If someone who was supposed to be dead was really alive...

Arnold's language lesson played back in her mind. *"That whole line would be read as 'the girl with hair the color of flowers.'"*

She stared at him. As he stood there before her with a heavy sword in hand, looking down at her, he was so beautiful it was like he'd stepped out of a painting.

"What color was your mother's hair?"

Several seconds passed before a serene smile appeared on Arnold's face. His eyes were still dark—a fathomless color, like the sea at night. Quietly, Arnold answered, "Faint purple, like violet."

Rishe gasped. The previous royal priestess *hadn't* died. She had likely been offered up as a hostage. The Holy Kingdom of Domana had given her to Galkhein, to Arnold's father, to prevent him from invading them.

"Your mother was the royal priestess who was supposed to have died..." In other words, Arnold himself inherited the blood of the priestess.

Bishop Schneider's words came back to her then: *"You must not marry Arnold Hein."*

If the Church wanted to kill Millia because she'd inherited the priestess's blood, then it would make sense that they'd also want to prevent any new children in the bloodline.

That's why Prince Arnold told the bishop I was nothing but a trophy wife!

He was saying that he had no intention of having a child with Rishe who could qualify as a priestess. His words were intended to prevent the Church from doing any harm to his future wife.

It was all to protect me.

In fact, the whole reason Arnold accompanied her to the Grand Basilica might have been to give the Church a warning. Yet Arnold had never spoken a word of that to Rishe.

"My father is likely behind the assassination attempts on the priestess."

Once again, Rishe gasped as Arnold spoke indifferently about Millia, his cousin. He then turned around and headed up the stairs. Rishe didn't sense Millia or the archbishop on this floor, and Arnold had likely noticed the same thing.

"You believe your father is involved in the assassination?"

"Not directly, but he's the cause of it."

Rishe followed Arnold, heading upstairs with him.

Without turning back to her, Arnold continued, "In exchange for not invading them, Galkhein formed a treaty with the Holy Kingdom of Domana twenty-two years ago."

"A treaty..."

The emperor of Galkhein hadn't spared the Holy Kingdom of Domana from invasion because he was a devout believer in the Church. He just used his military power to force them into a secret agreement. The Holy Kingdom itself became the emperor's hostage, along with the royal priestess who married him and Arnold, who'd inherited her precious blood.

"Part of the treaty was that any person qualified to become the priestess in the next twenty years be handed over to Galkhein."

"Then the reason Millia's been kept hidden is..."

"Not to protect her from the world at large but from my home country."

They passed by the entrance to the eighth floor and continued up the stairs toward the ninth. Rishe was almost winded, but she tried to keep Arnold from noticing.

"My father has made it clear he will destroy the Church if they break the treaty. The existence of the priestess goes against their agreement."

"That's why Leo said Galkhein would wipe out the Church!"

Arnold whirled around when he heard that. "So Leo was the priestess's protector, not her assassin?" There was no emotion in his voice. He spun forward again and muttered, "The Church isn't a monolith. Guess there's one faction trying to keep the royal priestess alive and another trying to kill her before Galkhein finds out about her."

"Is the archbishop trying to kill Lady Millia so that Galkhein has no reason to invade?"

"It's rather shortsighted of him to think they can murder her beneath our notice." His tone deliberate, Arnold went on, "They're holding the festival so he could call the priestess here and get her away from her guards."

Rishe's heart throbbed. She felt sick and dizzy, her anemic state worsening. Part of it was because of all the moving around, but there was another obvious cause right in front of her.

So much bloodlust!

The bloodthirstiness radiating from Arnold triggered an instinctive fear in Rishe. Her body was telling her that he was dangerous—that she had to get away from him as soon as possible. An unpleasant sweat welled up on her skin.

"The traps in the forest were made to look like some nearby hunters had put them there, but they were also attempts on her life. After all, the young priestess was likely the only person who would enter the forbidden forest." Arnold stopped in front of the door to the ninth floor. "But those traps almost cost you your life."

She shuddered at Arnold's low voice. "Your Highness! Please calm yourself! You're liable to create unnecessary victims at this rate."

"Unnecessary? Why?" Arnold headed for the door, saying, "The Church broke the treaty and openly displayed their will to resist. If they're going to come after our lives, I don't see how they could complain if we do the same."

"You just said yourself that they're not a monolith! They may all belong to the Church, but they don't all think the same way!"

Arnold's only response was to raise his leg and kick the heavy door open.

Instantly, arrows fell upon them like rain. Before Rishe could even put her guard up, Arnold stepped forward. He repelled all arrows with a single sweep of his sword.

He blocked them all in one swing!

There were a dozen or so bow-wielding monks in the large hall, guarding the altar behind them. They were completely panicked, but Arnold's eyes weren't even focused on them. He was looking only at the archbishop, who was dragging an unconscious Millia to the altar.

"There he is." Arnold's eyes were like a carnivorous beast's. "He's not going to kill the priestess on the altar, is he? That's almost funny." Arnold laughed, sounding truly amused. "Does the old man truly think that'll justify his actions? Ridiculous."

"Your Highness—"

"You stay here," he ordered. "Oliver."

"As you wish."

Rishe started; Oliver had crept up behind her at some point during their conversation.

I didn't even notice. Is my condition so bad that my senses have dulled this much?

She squeezed her fists. Before she could even call out to Arnold, he rushed into the room. Though she wanted to follow, Oliver's hand was clamped firmly on her shoulder. She faced him but had no energy to shake him off.

"Oliver! His Highness is going to kill the archbishop!"

"I'm sure he will. I wouldn't worry about it, though." Oliver smiled, the picture-perfect attendant. "The Church elders will doubtless excommunicate the archbishop if he does."

"But—"

"The existence of the royal priestess, their hiding her, the assassination attempts... I imagine they'll foist it all upon the archbishop and offer him up to the emperor to atone. Then they'll hand Lady Millia over to Galkhein and say, 'It's a little late, but our treaty still stands,' and that'll be that."

Rishe's head pounded. Bile rose in her throat.

"I'm sure this would have happened sooner or later. The emperor's interest was piqued when they announced they would resume the festival, you see. I think this will be a much more peaceful way to end things than the emperor going to war with the Church over Lady Millia's existence."

"Peaceful?!"

"However…" Oliver's perfect smile faded from his face, replaced by one that seemed forlorn. "If my lord kills several people in order to save his cousin, Lady Millia, I'm sure he'll only end up carrying more burdens."

"Oliver, you…"

"I'd quite like for you to help him if possible. Presumptuous of me to say so, I know, considering my lord doesn't wish for the same thing." With that, Oliver's hand left Rishe's shoulder.

Arnold charged toward the altar, avoiding and deflecting the monks' arrows. The closer he got, the more accurate their shots were, but that didn't slow him down.

He'll be there soon, but I've got other fish to fry!

The archbishop hoisted Millia up onto the altar.

I have to save Mistress Millia!

Arnold was fast, but he wouldn't make it in time. Rishe tightened her grip on the sacred tools in her hands: the royal priestess's bow, the holy artifact that should have been used in the festival rite.

I'm sorry, Mistress. Rishe took a deep breath. *Please let me borrow your sacred tools.*

"What are you doing?!" Oliver's eyes nearly popped out as Rishe nocked an arrow. "You're being reckless! The altar is too far; even a trained archer would have trouble making that shot!"

"This is all I've got." She stood with her feet shoulder-width apart and lined up her shot, aiming for the archbishop's legs. An arrow in the leg wouldn't kill him, but it would pin him in place and cause a *lot* of pain. If her arrow met its mark, he wouldn't be able to harm Millia.

"Lady Rishe, please!"

We're indoors, and there's no wind. No trees or brush in the way, and my target won't scurry like a wild animal.

Rishe took several deep breaths, honing her concentration to a fine point. She shut out all the sounds and voices around her, pulling the bowstring taut. Her hand hovered by her ear. She steadied it.

He'll be an easier target than the game in my fifth loop—my life as a hunter.

She didn't need to watch butterflies or birds to read the coming weather, climb trees to hide, conceal her presence, or track prey through mountains. At the end of her arrowhead, the archbishop was reaching for Millia.

Now!

At just the right moment, she let the arrow fly. It sped past Arnold, who whipped his head back at her for a second, then faced forward immediately after. A second later...

"Aaaahh!" The archbishop tumbled down from the altar, clutching his thigh.

Behind Rishe, Oliver gasped. "He was over a hundred meters away, but that shot was so accurate!"

"Take care of this!" Rishe thrust the sacred bow at Oliver and sprinted for the altar herself. For now, she had to pretend she wasn't sluggish and sick.

I've stopped the archbishop. Just one more thing left to do!

Arnold sauntered toward the archbishop, sword in hand. His sharp, clacking footsteps were amplified by the chamber's strained air. The bow-wielding monks scattered in all directions.

"Prince Arnold!" Rishe called, but he ignored her.

Doubled over on the steps leading to the altar, the archbishop cowered before Arnold, holding his injured leg. "Stay back!"

"Silence," Arnold snapped, his voice ice-cold. Rishe couldn't see his face, but she *could* see the archbishop's expression as he attempted to crawl away from Arnold. "I haven't permitted you to speak."

The archbishop wheezed in terror. Just what was he was seeing? His face was tense, pale, and twitching.

Arnold took a single glance at Millia atop the altar and said with disinterest, "The previous priestess's sister was supposed to be of poor health, wasn't she? It was deemed difficult for her to bear a child, so she wasn't subject to the treaty."

"I told you to stay away!"

"So then..." Arnold took his final step forward. He regarded the archbishop and quietly asked, "What is her daughter doing here?"

Deathly pale, the archbishop tried desperately to explain himself with wild gesticulations. "I was always against it!"

"Oh?"

"It's utter folly to defy Galkhein! Twenty-two years ago, I offered our precious royal priestess to your country to express my loyalty!"

Rishe's lips thinned into a line as she darted toward the altar. The archbishop continued to babble, ignoring Arnold's steely silence.

"But I couldn't just go against the cardinals. I only pretended to agree, and I waited ten years for this opportunity! If we let

Millia live, we won't be able to avoid conflict with Galkhein. That will lead to another war—the violent disruption of peace all around the world!"

"..."

"I may have gone against the cardinals, but I never intended to betray Galkhein! My decision to get rid of her was out of loyalty to you and your father, Your Highness!" The archbishop clasped his hands in front of his chest. "It was all for the sake of global peace!"

"..."

The archbishop prayed not to the goddess but to Arnold, voice quivering. "I beg you, please understand!"

One of the most prominent religious figures in the world was pleading with Arnold. His response was curt. "And why should I have to listen to your insipid prayers?"

The archbishop gaped at Arnold.

"I have no interest in any world of your creation. Unlike my father, I'm perfectly content to end you."

"Ugh!"

"This is extremely convenient." Arnold must have been smiling; Rishe knew it from the look on the archbishop's face. "The treaty gives me a legitimate excuse to get rid of you."

"N-no...!"

At last, she reached them. "Your Highness!" Rishe grabbed Arnold's sleeve and called out to him, out of breath. But Arnold didn't answer; he didn't even look her way. She said his name once again, as if in prayer. "Prince Arnold."

After several painful seconds, Arnold turned around, scowling. "Rishe. Don't tell me you're about to beg for his life."

"I'm afraid that's exactly what I'm going to do. I beseech you, please put your sword away!"

Arnold sneered at her. "You're just saying that because you were the only one who nearly died from all this."

"I..."

"You're too indifferent to your own safety. You act as if you've forgotten your own mortality."

On the inside, Rishe was sweating, but she made sure not to show it on her face. She looked Arnold in the eye and pleaded with him. "You cannot kill this man. Even if you save Lady Millia, killing the archbishop of the Crusade will inevitably spark strife with the Church!"

"Why should I care?" Arnold growled, shaking off her hand.

"Ah!"

She wanted to use her whole body to stop him, but any force she could muster probably wouldn't even slow him down. If she leaped in front of the archbishop, all Arnold had to do was push her aside.

He can't kill him. I don't want Prince Arnold to think that he can only use the same methods as his father to accomplish things.

If she let him kill the archbishop here, it would all be over. Rishe knew the future, after all. Arnold wasn't the sort of person who believed murder was the best way to solve a problem, yet he still moved toward the archbishop.

I'll have to distract him! I need to get him to stop thinking about how much he wants to kill the archbishop! How can I pull his attention away from his anger, even for a second?!

Arnold adjusted his grip on his sword to get it into position. The archbishop was completely petrified with fear. Rishe rifled through her thoughts for a solution.

What can I do? Think! What shocked me the most recently?

What had completely distracted her from everything she'd been thinking and feeling previously? The moment she asked herself that question, a vivid memory replayed in her mind.

Yes! That's it!

Now that she had a plan of action, there was no time to waste. She ran up to Arnold and reached for him. "Prince Arnold!"

Rishe threw her arms around his neck and used her weight to pull him closer, her eyes locked on to the exposed nape above his high collar. Then she brought her lips down on it.

"What are you—?!"

She opened her mouth wide and bit down hard on Arnold's neck.

"Huh?!" Arnold's dumbfounded voice was right in her ear.

The large room went completely quiet. Arnold's bloodlust wavered. At the same moment, his hand went to her hip, and Rishe released Arnold's neck with a gasp. Arnold's blue eyes considered Rishe from up close.

"What are you doing?" he asked with a glare. Although he didn't seem nearly as murderous, his face was somehow more frightening.

Oliver and the archbishop watched, mouths agape.

With Arnold's hand around her waist, Rishe blinked. "What am I doing?" A beat. "Oh no, did it hurt?!"

"I didn't say anything about that!" Arnold raised his voice uncharacteristically, and Rishe flinched in surprise.

As long as it didn't hurt him, then it's fine.

With a sigh of relief, she reached up to touch Arnold's cheek. She peered up at him in earnest and said, "I was just trying to make you look at me." Holding his face in her hands, she looked deep into his blue eyes. They were so close she could see herself in them. "The archbishop's plan ended in failure."

"..."

"As long as you're here, his fear will immobilize him. There's nothing he can do anymore." Rishe side-eyed the archbishop, who flinched in terror. He was completely frozen and probably wouldn't even be able to stand.

Still, Arnold narrowed his eyes. "There is no justice in anything this man said." His voice was even lower than usual. "I already know he's distantly related to the priestess. Killing her direct descendant would benefit him. Do you think a saint who kills a child for his own selfish reasons deserves to live?" He gently placed his hand over Rishe's. "If we tell the cardinals of the Church about this, they'll happily offer him up to us. Even if some of the cardinals were involved in the assassination, they'll cut him off and feign ignorance."

Arnold gently interlaced their fingers in hers and drew her hand away from his face, but Rishe didn't break eye contact. Feeling a little despondent, she said, "Even if that's true, then it's all the more reason not to. You shouldn't have to kill *anyone* if it's not what you want."

The prince's brow lifted in surprise. "I do want to kill this man."

"No, you don't," Rishe asserted. "You aren't even angry for your own sake. It's for me and Lady Millia, I'm sure of it." *And perhaps his mother too.*

Rishe knew the Arnold in front of her well. He was both the brutal crown prince who was feared on battlefields in the past and the cold-blooded tyrant who was dreaded in the future.

"You said that I was too indifferent to my own safety. Well, to me, it seems as though you're too indifferent to your own emotions, Prince Arnold."

"What are you—"

"Please," she said gently, stopping him. This time, she didn't touch his cheek. She looked down, reached out to the hand grasping his sword, and gripped his sleeve. "I don't want a kind person like you to keep acting as if killing people doesn't affect you."

While she could no longer see Arnold's expression, she knew that if she raised her head now, her voice would start to shake.

I can't. She was making a one-sided demand of Arnold, but she couldn't let herself act so pathetic before him.

Rishe took a shallow breath to calm her wavering heart, then met Arnold's eyes. "If you kill him, it will all be over here. It will be much more difficult to ascertain the full extent of his plans and everyone who was involved in them."

"..."

"But since we have him right where we want him, it's more like you to make effective use of everything you have at your disposal. Isn't that right, Prince Arnold Hein?"

Arnold held her gaze and asked, "Do you really think he'll confess to all of his schemes?"

"Yes, I believe he will."

"Just what about him is so trustworthy to you?"

"It's not him I trust, but you, Prince Arnold," Rishe said.

Arnold's brow furrowed ever so slightly before he heaved a deep sigh. He turned back to the archbishop, transferred his sword from his right hand to his left, and swung it down.

"Eek!"

The sound of crumbling marble filled the room. Arnold had embedded his sword into the floor next to the archbishop. Rishe knew he no longer intended to kill the man, but even she shuddered.

Arnold studied the archbishop, who was quaking and unable to speak. "In deference to my wife, I'll spare your life. Never forget what you owe to her."

"I...I-I under—"

"I hope you're not under some foolish misconception that you've been completely spared, though. I'm going to squeeze every single piece of information out of you no matter what it takes." Arnold went down on one knee and loomed over the archbishop. "I'm going to make sure you wish you'd died today."

Beside him, goosebumps erupted across Rishe's skin. Arnold exuded more bloodlust than when he was holding his sword. She found herself rooted to the spot.

Arnold stood, wrenched his sword from the cracked floor, and sheathed it. At that moment, a dozen or so people stormed up to the entrance.

More Church soldiers?! Rishe wheeled around right as the big doors swung open. Standing at the front of the pack was Bishop Schneider, who should have been unconscious on a lower floor. *What is he doing here? No, there's no time for that. We must deal with this before Mistress Millia wakes up!*

As Rishe tensed, Arnold held a hand up. "Prince Arnold?" she asked, confused.

Ever composed, he replied, "He's not working with the archbishop. I suspect they've been enemies for quite some time."

"Erm… Enemies, you say?"

Schneider looked around the room and called out to the monks behind him. "Look! His Highness Prince Arnold of our allied nation of Galkhein has saved the royal priestess!"

The monks raised a cheer.

"Oh." Rishe couldn't help but gape. Frankly, she'd been beside herself with worry. After all, Millia was unconscious, the archbishop was in a terrorized stupor, and Arnold had wielded his sword left and right, knocking out all the attacking monks on his way here.

I was afraid they wouldn't believe that we're trying to save Mistress Millia and we'd make an enemy of the Church. I suppose I have Bishop Schneider to thank?

The monks ran over and tied up the archbishop. One after the other, they expressed their gratitude to Prince Arnold.

"Your Highness! We were only able to save Lady Millia thanks to you!"

"I don't know how we could possibly repay you!"

After frowning in deep discomfort, Arnold wordlessly glanced at Schneider. Beside him stood Leo, who must have freed himself from Rishe's binds. He met her eyes, sheepish.

Rishe sighed with relief. *Bishop Schneider must have assigned Leo to protect Mistress Millia.*

Another man scrambled into the room, white as a sheet. "Millia!"

"Please wait, Your Grace." Schneider grabbed the duke by his arm. "The archbishop may still have some minions lurking about. You should stay—"

"Sorry, but please let me go!" The duke jerked out of Schneider's grip and took off. He didn't even notice Arnold or Rishe. He dashed straight to the monks who had lifted Millia and scooped her up in his arms. "Millia!"

Millia slowly opened her eyes and blinked up at him. "Papa...?" After a few seconds, her eyes finally focused, and she threw her arms around the duke's neck. "Papa!"

"Ah, you poor thing! That must have been terrifying! Are you hurt, my darling?!" Holding Millia close, the distraught duke apologized over and over. "I'm such an idiot! I didn't even know who to trust! I believed the archbishop and handed you over! You're more important to me than my own life, and I couldn't protect you! I'm sorry!"

Millia sobbed into her father's chest.

"I'm a failure of a father. There's no way you can stay with—"

"No! No, no!" Millia shook her head. The duke looked down at her, confused. "I had a dream after the archbishop gave me that medicine. I dreamed I was here at the Grand Basilica and a bunch of dangerous things fell on me and you saved me, Papa."

"I did?"

"You got hurt because of it, but then you lied about it forever after, saying it was 'cause of an old illness you had. See? You protected me, even in my dream!" Millia clung to the duke, sobbing uncontrollably. "I knew I would be safe 'cause I was dreaming of you, Papa. So...so...please don't cry!"

"Oh, Millia!"

"I'm sorry for worrying you, Papa. But..." Millia's voice was ever so quiet and forlorn. "I promise I'll be a good girl, so please keep being my papa."

"Of course I will!" the duke shouted to assuage his daughter's fears. "I never want you to forget, no matter how naughty you are, that I'll always love you and be on your side!"

"Papa!"

Millia's sobs echoed through the room. In Rishe's fourth loop, she worked hard to keep Millia from crying, but now she felt only relief upon seeing the tears on the young girl's face. She glanced at Arnold. "That's an awfully complicated face you're making."

"The duke and the priestess aren't even blood relations, are they?" Arnold, who *was* Millia's blood relative, frowned as he watched them. "Why is he so concerned with the priestess's well-being? I don't understand it at all."

"Oh? Didn't you say on our way to the Grand Basilica that 'blood ties have nothing to do with how well two people get along'?"

Arnold challenged her with his eyes. At the time, Arnold meant that blood relations didn't mean two people would bond, but Rishe had flipped his words to mean the opposite.

"You were exactly right. Blood ties have nothing to do with it."

"..."

"They may not be blood-related, but those two are, without a doubt, father and daughter."

Arnold looked dissatisfied for a few seconds, then exhaled. "Whatever. Oliver!"

"Yes, my lord. I'm prepared to receive my punishment." The silver-haired attendant slipped over with a sunny smile. Usually, Oliver only referred to Arnold as his lord when there was no one to overhear him. "I was ordered to hold Lady Rishe back, but I let her go. I apologize. With all due respect, however, I believe my decision was the right one."

"..."

"I could never have imagined the way Lady Rishe would stop you. Hee hee hee hee..."

"..."

"I only regret that I couldn't see your face when it happened. Such a pit—oww!"

He kicked him! Rishe went wide-eyed as Oliver hunched over his shin. Arnold had wordlessly given him a vicious kick. She was reminded that Arnold only seemed to act like a young man of nineteen around Oliver.

"Are you all right, Oliver?!"

"Let's go, Rishe. You need to rest immediately. I don't care about anything else."

"Huh? But, um, Oliver looks like he's in a lot of pain."

"Leave him be. If you won't come with me, then I'll carry you."

"Eep!" Rishe gave Oliver a silent apology and followed Arnold. Then her legs gave out from under her.

Seeing Rishe collapse, Arnold immediately bent down.

"Ack!" This situation was a familiar one to Rishe, so she yelped, "N-not the princess carry, please!"

"No?"

She thrust her hands out at Arnold in protest. "I can walk by myself; I'm fine! If I just rest for a minute, I—eek!"

Rishe blanched as she was lifted into the air. *Your Highness, noooo!*

"You just don't want to be carried sideways, right?"

She thought she deserved an award for not screaming. Arnold carried her upright, unlike the last time. He had his left arm under her butt while his right arm supported her back. Rishe was forced to clutch his shoulders to steady herself.

His Highness is slim, so why does he have so much arm strength?! And is it just me or are there more parts of us touching this way? It's actually even more embarrassing than being carried like a princess!

Since he was lifting her up so high, she naturally had to look down on Arnold—which should have been a nice change, but she was too flustered to enjoy the moment. The monks too were downright flabbergasted—their eyes nearly popped out of their sockets. Rishe's cheeks burned from the attention.

"Prince Arnold!" she pleaded. "I'm really fine, so could you just...please!"

"I'm not putting you down."

"Arrrgh!"

Rishe was helpless; she knew Arnold would not be dissuaded. Her head was on a swivel in search of someone who could save her, but Oliver, the only one likely to even comment on the situation, was still doubled over on the floor. If she'd known this would happen, she wouldn't have abandoned him.

While Rishe stewed in her regret, Arnold walked off, indifferent to her discomfort. Plus, he was irritated. "You ran around without waiting for your stamina to recover. You're always pushing yourself."

"Wh-whose fault is that this time?!"

Arnold huffed and muttered with self-derision, "Mine." At that, Rishe felt a twinge in her chest.

Bishop Schneider cut off their path. "Prince Arnold, do you have a moment?"

"As you can see, my wife is in rather poor health. Anything you wish to say to me can wait."

What do you mean, "As you can see"?!

The prince headed straight for the stairs. He made it clear that he didn't intend to stop, so Schneider didn't follow him. Instead, he gave Rishe a serene look. His warning came to mind.

"You must not marry Arnold Hein."

Rishe clung to Arnold and set her jaw, making her resolution clear. The bishop's eyes widened in astonishment, and he bowed deeply to Rishe.

"What is it?" Arnold asked. Rishe couldn't see his face anymore.

"You might lose your balance on the stairs if I don't hold tight, and that would be dangerous."

"Hah!" Had he seen through her lie? Oddly, Arnold sounded amused. He patted her lightly on the back as if soothing a child. "I won't let you get hurt no matter what happens, so don't worry."

"H-how about you worry about your *own* safety!"

"I don't want to hear that from you."

The exchange rubbed her the wrong way, but she couldn't argue in this position. She was too distracted by the thrumming of her heart and the burning in her cheeks.

Rishe stroked the mark she'd left on Arnold's neck, attempting to be casual about it. Then she squeezed her eyes shut and prayed all the way down the stairs for Arnold to put her down soon.

***

Arnold carried Rishe all the way to her room and heaved her into bed. Normally, he was very good about granting Rishe's requests, but this time he ignored each and every one of them, be it "I'd like to help clean up a bit" or "Could I see how Lady Millia is doing?"

Having no other choice, Rishe behaved herself and rested. Her stamina had recovered by the next morning, whereupon she accompanied Arnold to see Bishop Schneider.

"The Church cardinals have always been divided into different factions." Schneider's gray hair was combed back neatly, but he also had heavy bags under his eyes. It was clear that he'd been hard at work since yesterday.

"One faction raised Lady Millia in secret, trying to keep her from Galkhein. The other feared Galkhein and tried to erase Lady Millia, like the archbishop."

Rishe frowned at this distressing news. "So there were several people who sought to harm Lady Millia."

"Yes. They were by far the minority, however. The royal priestess is the heir to the goddess's bloodline and the object of our faith."

That was a relief, but she still couldn't completely trust Schneider. Arnold seemed to feel the same way.

"Sure seems like you allowed the object of your faith to act as bait."

Seated beside Rishe on the couch, Arnold was resting his chin in hand on the armrest. His sword was nearby, propped up against the other side of the armrest, when it should have been left outside the room with Oliver.

"If you really wanted to protect the priestess, you shouldn't have summoned her to a place within the archbishop's reach. If the majority truly wished to raise her in secret, then it should have been easy to keep her out of the public eye."

It was exactly as Arnold said. As the archbishop's aide, if Schneider had caught wind of his plans, then he never should have let any of this happen.

"One faction wanted to raise the priestess in secret and another wanted to eliminate her. I'm still not clear on which *you* belong to."

"Actually, I don't belong to either."

"Oh?" Arnold said, though his face bore not a lick of interest.

Schneider clasped his hands over his knees and leaned forward. "I know that my plan put Lady Millia in danger, but I needed to swiftly remove the archbishop from the picture. To that end, I had to prove that he was actively planning on eliminating Lady Millia. I needed decisive proof."

"And that's why you let the archbishop attack Lady Millia in front of all those monks?" Rishe asked.

Schneider hung his head. "Frankly, I didn't account for the possibility of the crown prince of Galkhein visiting during this period." He seemed genuinely dejected. "I considered the archbishop our enemy, but I thought *you* were our enemies too. Even if I could uncover the archbishop's plot, everything would still be over if Galkhein's crown prince found out about the royal priestess."

"Is that why you sent Leo to stop me?"

"He reported to me that you likely had some sort of martial training, Lady Rishe. I didn't think you'd defeat the most talented child from my 'orphanage' quite so handily, though." Schneider's smile was rueful as he said, "He still has a long way to go."

From the way he spoke, it seemed Leo had been telling the truth when he'd said the bishop wasn't like a father to him. Schneider was more like a teacher watching over his student. The archbishop must not have known about the orphanage's true purpose.

"Why was Leo in the forest near the traps?"

"To inform me where the archbishop had set them. I couldn't easily enter the forest myself since the archbishop had declared it off-limits."

Leo's actions could be written off as simple, innocent mischief. Everything Schneider said seemed reasonable, but Rishe couldn't bring herself to accept the man's words wholeheartedly.

"The archbishop thought Lady Millia might enter the forest, being a bit of a troublemaker, and left the traps there to make her death look like an accident," Rishe mused. "Lady Millia *did* end up in danger in the forest. Knowing it could happen, why did you leave the traps there?"

"Leo should have protected her before she was in any danger. He took his eyes off her, so Lady Millia entered the forest and put herself in danger." Schneider gazed at Rishe for a moment before continuing, "If the worst had happened, I would have punished Leo myself and offered up my own life to the goddess in apology."

Rishe's face tightened. In the future, when Leo had been beaten so badly that he'd lost an eye, there was no one named Schneider among the leadership of the Church and someone else had been archbishop. That must have been the aftermath of the worst-case scenario.

"Save your excuses," Arnold told Schneider, voice low. "What you need to explain is why you set up this whole situation, including your plans for the priestess and your stance on my father."

"You would hear what I have to say?"

"Drop the humble act. You're going to be the next archbishop, aren't you?"

"That depends entirely on you, Your Highness."

Arnold knit his brows.

"As I said before, there are several factions in the Church. One wanted to keep the priestess alive and hidden from Galkhein; the other wanted to kill her before Galkhein discovered her identity. Originally, I was in the first camp, but that's no longer the case."

"What exactly is it that you want, Bishop Schneider?" Rishe asked.

"I would like for us to form an alliance." Schneider chuckled at Rishe's look of surprise. "Not with Galkhein and His Majesty the Emperor, but with you two—Prince Arnold Hein and soon-to-be Princess Rishe."

"I..."

"I'd very much like for Lady Millia's existence to remain hidden from His Majesty. I would also like to repay you in whatever way I can if I become the next archbishop."

Rishe found all this quite unexpected. The only reason she'd visited the Grand Basilica when she had was to meet Millia. She thought she could avoid the future war if she formed a relationship with the Crusade Church, which had influence all around the world, or Millia, who would be its royal priestess. She just wanted to avoid the future where Arnold burned down churches and tried to kill Millia.

In all the lives I've lived up until now, Prince Arnold has been against the Church. If we can really forge an alliance with them now, it's sure to change the future. But...

Her gaze flicked to Arnold, who was regarding Schneider with a look of absolute disgust.

"An alliance? You don't know your place, Schneider. No matter what you people wish for, I already know about the priestess."

"It's exactly as you say."

"The Church's power means nothing to me. Meanwhile, this is a matter of life and death to you. If you really have the time to make such laughable propositions, then you should be spending it groveling a little more sincerely, don't you think?"

"Prince Arnold," Rishe said, but Arnold didn't spare her a glance.

The bishop's face paled. "As I said, my fate depends on you, Your Highness." He bowed his head as if offering his neck. "If lowering my head will convince you, then I don't mind if it separates from my body and falls to the ground. I leave the decision to you."

"It would be a good show of bravado if you weren't trembling. That goddess of yours isn't going to save you, you know."

"I exercise my faith not to receive salvation from the goddess but to serve Her. If I can save the goddess's child with my life, then it has served its purpose."

Arnold prepared to retort just as the door flew open.

An adorable girl poked her head in. "Lady Rishe!" Millia burst into the room, a white flower crown atop her head and her eyes positively sparkling.

Arnold glared at Oliver, but the attendant just bowed and stepped back outside.

"Lady Millia! The festival is about to start! Are you all ready?" Rishe asked, embracing her.

Millia's smile resembled a flower in full bloom. "Yes, everything's perfect!"

Even after her harrowing experience, Millia had asked Schneider and her father if the festival could continue. The duke initially refused, but Millia dug her heels in. Apparently, when her father explained her heritage, this exchange had followed:

"I'm the real royal priestess, right? Then I need to perform my duty."

"Millia..."

"I want everyone to see that I can do it—that includes Mama and you too, Papa, since you've protected me all this time."

The duke had broken down after that, and the festival was scheduled to resume shortly.

Millia now donned the royal priestess's white dress.

"How are you feeling?"

"I was really sleepy yesterday, but now I'm fine! I heard that as soon as the festival ends, you'll be having the annulment ceremony for your previous engagement, and then you'll be returning to Galkhein."

Rishe nodded with a sad smile. "Yes, we're ready to head back as soon as I'm finished." Her trip to the Grand Basilica had been quite unreasonable in the first place. They still had a lot of wedding preparations to attend to, and she couldn't keep eating up so much of Arnold's time.

"I'll miss you, Lady Rishe!" Millia hung her head tearfully, and Rishe felt a twinge in her heart.

"And I you, Lady Millia."

I always knew I wouldn't be able to spend this life at Mistress Millia's side.

In her heart, Millia would always be Rishe's little mistress, whom she loved and respected deeply. Although she could be a stubborn little troublemaker, the girl was adorable and incredibly kind. Rishe had watched over Millia from age eleven until she was married at fifteen. All the while, she had loved the girl like a sister. *But I can't go back to that life, no matter how much I may miss her.*

"Say, Lady Rishe?" Milla squeezed Rishe's hand with her tiny fingers. "Even if we can't see each other much after this, um..."

"Yes?"

"Can I think of you like a big sister?"

For a moment, Rishe was worried Millia noticed her astonishment. She bent down to hide a joy so big, she was teary-eyed. Then she stroked Millia's cheek, red with embarrassment, and beamed brightly.

"I'd be delighted to have a sister like you, Lady Millia."

"Oh!" Millia exclaimed as Rishe wrapped her up in a hug. When she pulled back again, they mirrored each other's happy grins.

Millia then turned to Arnold. "Your Highness!"

Arnold just stared at her, but Millia didn't flinch. She pinched her dress's hem and curtsied before telling him, "Papa—I mean, my father—told me that you saved me, Your Highness. Thank you so much."

Rishe's gaze slid to Arnold, and she felt herself sweat. Millia was Arnold's cousin. She didn't know that, but Arnold was bound to feel something about it.

I do think he was concerned for Mistress Millia in his own way, but he most likely has no intent to reveal that they're family.

Eyes still frosty, Arnold told Millia, "I was merely granting my wife's wish. Nothing more."

"I see." Millia's shoulders slumped, but she quickly brightened at a sudden realization. "You're going to marry Lady Rishe, though, aren't you?!"

"What about it?"

"Then you'll be my big brother!"

Arnold's face morphed into a full-on scowl. Rishe burst out laughing.

"What's so funny?"

"Nothing, I just think Lady Millia's exactly right! After all, you're going to become my husband, aren't you, Your Highness?" Rishe stroked Millia's hair and gazed into her honey-colored eyes. "Please think of us as family. Me *and* Prince Arnold."

"Yay! I'm gonna do my very best during the festival rite!" Millia hopped in place, giddy, and smiled at Arnold. "Please come and watch too, Prince Arnold!"

"..."

"Anyway, sorry for interrupting!" Millia chirped before she scurried out of the room. Leo could be heard scolding her beyond the door, but his voice gradually faded.

"Being born as the priestess could only be a burden for her, and yet..." Arnold muttered.

Perhaps in response, Schneider told Arnold, "I must confess, I told Lady Rishe the other day that she shouldn't marry you. I didn't think she knew the truth of your parentage."

I didn't exactly hear about it; I pretty much figured it out myself.

To be honest, she hadn't the faintest idea at the time, so Schneider's assumption was correct. She didn't need to amend that point, though.

"You should not bring children with the goddess's blood into this world without knowing. It will one day lead to great upheaval. If you happen to have a girl, the Church will be prepared to go to war to get their hands on that child."

"Hmph."

"It would be cruel to be the mother of such a child without knowing the truth. But the future crown princess of Galkhein is made of much stronger stuff than I was expecting."

Rishe was unsure how to take the compliment. "I'm afraid you give me too much credit."

"If possible, I would like to forge a new relationship between Galkhein and the Church with the two of you. That way, children of the priestess's bloodline do not have to shoulder such a burden—not just Lady Millia, but any *future* children as well."

"Is that so?" Rishe murmured. She studied Arnold again, but there was no change in his expression.

Prince Arnold will set the Church aflame in the future. But how does he feel about it right now?

Was it hatred of the Church that drove his actions? Rishe couldn't answer just by puzzling it out. She still knew nothing of what happened between Arnold and his mother.

A knock on the door interrupted her musings.

"Bishop Schneider, I apologize for the interruption, but it's almost time for the festival."

"Wait! Your Highness, please." This was Schneider's last stand. If he let Arnold return to Galkhein, there would be no further chance for negotiation.

Arnold clicked his tongue and stared down at Schneider. "What do you want? If you're needed elsewhere, hurry up and go."

"But, Your Highness, I—"

"I'll keep the priestess a secret from my father," he said, and Schneider gasped.

Rishe was equally stunned. "Really?!"

"That was always my intention. I don't want him making a mess over her existence." Irritated, Arnold added, "It'll be easier to prevent that if I cooperate with the Church leadership."

Schneider opened his mouth, but whatever he intended to say must've gotten stuck in his throat. Some color was finally returning to his face; Rishe found herself sighing with relief as well.

"Is that all right? As you said earlier, you don't stand to benefit much from the agreement."

"I'll benefit. I don't need the power of the Church, but if I have it, I'll find ways to use it."

"Then…?"

"We don't need to go into details here." Still scowling, Arnold repeated his earlier words. "Did you not hear me? Hurry up and go."

A monk's voice came from outside. "We really should start preparing, Bishop."

Schneider stood and bowed once more to Arnold. "I will not forget the kindness you have shown me. May the goddess bless the both of you."

"Keep your blessings. I don't want anything to do with them."

Schneider's wry smile returned, and he addressed Rishe. "Then may you have His Highness's blessings as well, Lady Rishe."

Smiling back, Rishe accepted. "Thank you, Bishop Schneider."

When Schneider left the room, Rishe and Arnold were alone.

Adjusting her position on the couch, Rishe asked, "You're not pushing yourself, are you?"

Arnold scrunched his face, puzzled. "I'm not."

"Well, good."

"Why would you ask that? You'd prefer to have a relationship with the Church too if it means a relationship with the priestess, right?"

"Well, of course, but…" Rishe pursed her lips. "I don't want you to do anything against your will."

Arnold huffed and leaned on the backrest. "I'm not totally against it."

"Seriously?"

"I said the same thing to the bishop, didn't I? Being in the Church's good graces means nothing to me, but I'm content to make use of it."

I just hope you won't make use of it for war.

Although she wasn't entirely happy about Arnold's decision, Rishe considered it a small victory. Arnold wasn't the only one who would use whatever was at his disposal to his advantage. Rishe now had a connection to the Church as well, and she intended to make good use of it to avoid the war.

"Good. I think Lady Millia will be happy about this too."

Arnold's mouth bent in a frown. "I don't like children."

"My, Oliver will be upset if he hears you say that."

"Why?"

"He seems to think you shouldn't say such things to your future wife."

"Hah!" Arnold laughed goadingly. He tilted Rishe's head in his direction. "I didn't think you had the resolve for that."

"Hnnh?!" Rishe hadn't expected this turn of conversation and made a strange noise in her consternation. "Wh-what do you mean, 'resolve'?"

"You're talking about an heir, aren't you? Schneider was just talking about our future children as well."

Rishe squeaked, and her mind went blank at the sudden change in the room's atmosphere.

Arnold chuckled. "You really didn't get it."

"No, I-I did! I mean it, really!"

"Oh yeah?"

She *had* known the bishop was referring to their children; she just hadn't been considering it in such practical terms. It was a mere hypothetical in her mind.

The prince smiled at her, drinking in her fluster. "You knew, yet you set up different rooms for us in the detached palace."

That's where I went wrong?!

Arnold had just pointed out a rather distressing truth, but she couldn't let him know the extent of her panic. Sight spinning, she desperately fished for rebuttals.

"That's because you promised at first not to lay a finger on me, Prince Arnold!"

"And you annulled that agreement several days ago, so I am no longer under such an obligation."

"Ugh..."

Arnold's finger traced the band around her left ring finger.

Wh-wh-what do I do?!

"I'm teasing you too much." Arnold snickered, seeing how beside herself Rishe was. "Don't worry." He mussed her hair a little and said, "Even after we're married, I won't take advantage of you."

"Huh?" Rishe blinked, scrutinizing Arnold's sea-colored eyes. "You won't?"

"I won't."

When he stated his intentions so plainly, she realized, *That's right. Prince Arnold proposed to me with some sort of ulterior motive in mind.* She took a deep breath when she remembered that. *He's not looking for me to play the role of a real wife.*

Oddly enough, the thought both relieved and gnawed at her. Rishe tilted her head in confusion as a dull ache settled in her chest.

Oblivious to Rishe's consternation, Arnold leaned back once more and loosed a yawn.

Seeing him act so defenseless, Rishe decided to put her own emotions aside for the moment. "Are you tired?"

"Yeah." His tone was gentler than usual.

He made sure that I got enough rest, but Prince Arnold has been rather busy, hasn't he?

The night before last, she'd made him sleep in the same bed as her too. Arnold was very sensitive to other people's presence, so he likely hadn't gotten a proper night's rest then.

"Would you like to nap until the festival starts?"

Arnold looked at her for a time. "I suppose so." He then stretched out on the couch, laying his head on Rishe's lap.

"Y-Your Highness!"

"Lend me your lap. I'll take a nap here."

Rishe gulped. She didn't *mind*, per se. They were just a bit close, and Arnold's head was resting on her thighs, which felt strange—but what was even stranger was that she wasn't bothered by it at all.

"If you don't want me to, I can move."

"I-It's not that, I just...have to tell Oliver."

"Leave him posted in the hall outside."

"Just leave him there?"

"He's been disobeying my orders too much lately." So he said, but Rishe was fairly certain that everything Oliver did, he did for his lord. "Is that your only issue?"

"Th-there's one more. Won't I make an uncomfortable pillow?"

"Why do you think that?"

"I just do." She couldn't say more than that. Thinking of yesterday morning embarrassed her.

Arnold must have remembered the same thing. He looked up at Rishe and said, "I slept well the night before last." Then he blinked more languidly than usual. "I didn't have any strange dreams. That's rare."

"Goodness..." She couldn't argue with that. Really, he should get to sleep in a real bed, no matter how brief, instead of napping here. By himself! However, Rishe was unable to muster up even these reasonable suggestions.

The prince gazed at her as she made an awkward face. "What were you dreaming about?"

"What?"

"Late at night, I was checking your condition, and...you rubbed your cheek against my hand and smiled."

"Huh?!" Rishe knew exactly what she'd been dreaming about. Even though she always dreamed of her past lives, that had been the first time since her loops began that she had a different sort of dream. She'd dreamed of *this* life, her life after meeting him.

"Hmm?"

Rishe let out a tiny squeal in response, screwing up her face. She couldn't possibly tell him the truth. "I-It's a secret."

"A secret, eh? I'm jealous."

"Don't lie." She sulked, covering Arnold's eyes. Since his eyelashes were long, they tickled against her palm. "Please rest already."

"Got it."

Only five minutes or so later, Arnold's breathing slowed. After ensuring he was truly asleep, Rishe removed her hand. Then she brushed her fingers against Arnold's lips.

There was that ache in her chest again.

* * *

The festival rite was executed with dignified grandeur. A beautifully dressed Millia stood before the altar, where Schneider served in the archbishop's place. Millia offered the sacred bow and arrow to the goddess and sang a beautiful song of dedication. She looked at once adorable and impressive, and she performed even more wonderfully than she had in her rehearsal. Rishe was fervently applauding the girl in her mind. Arnold, who watched from beside her, neither praised the affair nor made pithy gripes. For that, Rishe had to smile.

After the festival ended, Rishe continued where she'd had to leave off in her engagement annulment ceremony. She started before noon, and around two in the afternoon, her engagement with Dietrich was officially annulled. She had a light meal afterward, rushed to get ready for the ride home, and set out for the carriage. Arnold stood waiting by the carriage door.

"Thank you for waiting, Prince Arnold!"

"You don't need to hurry so much," Arnold said, but the inn where they would spend the night was two hours away. If they didn't leave soon, they would still be in the thick of the woods at sunset.

All their Imperial Guards were present as well. They'd been staying in a nearby village for the last four days, since they couldn't enter the Grand Basilica. While Rishe greeted them, she noticed a red-haired boy.

"Leeeo!" she said in a singsong voice.

"Ack!"

"What's up? Did you decide to come with us to Galkhein after all?"

Leo grimaced. "No. I just wanted to learn about Galkhein's fighting style up until the last possible minute."

It seemed Leo had been asking Arnold's Imperial Guards for advice. There was a small piece of gauze pasted to his face.

"How was Prince Arnold's training?"

"It was amazing."

While Rishe performed the engagement annulment ceremony, Arnold summoned Leo and gave him the promised sword lesson. The prince was plenty busy himself, but he'd still found time to teach. Leo had gotten a full lesson, but he didn't seem worn out at all; in fact, he seemed more energetic than Rishe had ever seen him.

"I'll absorb everything he taught me. Even after you guys leave, I'll get Schneider to give me more training."

"Hee hee hee. Motivation suits you." All the anxiety Rishe felt toward Leo evaporated. It helped that the reason he wanted to be strong wasn't to kill but to protect. She knew it wasn't her place to worry about him, but she was glad to have her fears dispelled anyway.

"Take care of yourself, Leo." Rishe knelt and met his stare, sincere in her wish. "Don't get hurt. Learn a lot, meet a lot of people, and expand your horizons."

In Rishe's head, she saw the Leo from her sixth loop. That Leo had escaped from Schneider and fled to another country, always seeming so angry at himself. The eyes with which he watched Rishe and the other knights train were those of someone whose goals were out of reach.

"I'll be thrilled if you keep on smiling even after you grow up."

Leo's brow bunched in confusion. "I don't really understand the things you say," he said, eyes downcast. "But practicing with Prince Arnold made me happy, and so did walking in the forest with you."

"Oh, Leo..."

"Not *that* much in the forest, though." He averted his eyes, and Rishe laughed. She was glad to hear that he wasn't suffering in his training to be a strong bodyguard.

"I must go. Just ask Prince Arnold if you ever decide you want to be a knight."

"No way. I want to be freer than a knight."

"Freer?" He must've been referring to a knight's social status. *True, it's probably a lot easier to get around as someone's bodyguard rather than a knight.*

With a huff, the boy declared, "I'm gonna be someone who travels freely through thick forests with a rope and fights with throwing knives and bows and arrows!" He stuck his tongue out at Rishe, face tomato-red, then bowed to Arnold and ran off.

And he's gone.

"Rishe."

"Oh! Yes!" She stood when Arnold called her and stepped up to the carriage. Arnold took her hand and led her inside, then boarded and sat across from her. After that, the carriage began to move.

"I take it there were no issues during your ceremony."

"Yes. Sorry it took so long, but it's finally done with."

"Good." Arnold set his chin in his hand and casually watched the Grand Basilica through the window.

Rishe looked not at the scenery outside but at Arnold. How did he feel, looking at that place that had so much to do with his late mother?

I wonder if I dredged up some unpleasant feelings by bringing him here.

Knowing what she did now, she fully believed Arnold had come to protect her. He was worried that the Church would do something to his fiancée, so he'd gone so far as to order them to keep their distance outside of her ceremony.

Even though I'm trying to get in the way of his plans.

In a way, she was working against him to try to prevent the war. If Arnold knew, how would he feel?

Since she was staring at him so openly, Arnold returned her gaze. His slender fingers reached out to her as well. He brushed her bangs away and touched her forehead.

"My fever's gone," Rishe said tentatively.

Nonchalant, he replied, "I've decided not to believe your evaluations of your own health."

"Urk!" That wounded her. It wasn't like Rishe was trying to lie. She frowned and hung her head, studying Arnold through her eyelashes. "What is your evaluation then, Prince Arnold?"

"You seem fine. Your complexion has improved." Arnold withdrew his hand and looked out the window once more. His expressionless face was even more unreadable than usual.

"Um, Your Highness?"

"Hmm?"

Wanting to make her thoughts a reality, Rishe asked, "Do you mind if we sit next to each other, rather than across?"

Arnold was taken aback.

Rishe's chest throbbed with pain, and she blurted, "N-never mind, across is fine! Right, I'm sure you have paperwork to do again, like on our way here!"

"No." Arnold let his gaze drop and patted the seat next to him.

At that, Rishe's eyes lit up. She stood carefully and Arnold held out a helping hand. With his assistance, she spun around and plopped down next to him.

"What are you scheming this time?"

"Well, you see..." She tucked Arnold's hair behind his ear. The moment Arnold's attention was focused on her left hand, she performed a trick with her right. "Ta-da!"

A pink flower crown appeared right before Arnold's eyes. Judging by his expression, she had succeeded in stunning him. With a satisfied smile, Rishe adorned his head with the flowers.

"Did that surprise you?"

"It did."

"Good! I was so frustrated that you saw through my trick on the way here, I practiced at the Grand Basilica."

The flower crown suited Arnold's beautiful features well—though she was sure he'd scowl if she told him that.

"The flower crowns they hand out during the festival are supposed to be blessings from the goddess."

"Oh, come on."

"I'm sure you'd be quick to spurn the goddess's blessing, right, Your Highness? That's why I made this one myself."

Rishe didn't think this would serve as an apology for dragging him out here, but she wanted to be of help to him in any way she could. She hoped the beauty and sweet aroma of the flowers might comfort him.

"This is your blessing, then?"

"Ugh… I'm not sure that you could call it anything that overblown."

Arnold huffed a laugh. Seeing him smile up close caused a sharp throb in her chest. But before she could reflect on that, Arnold said, "I just can't beat you."

Rishe blinked. She didn't understand. "I don't think I've ever won against you, Prince Arnold."

"That's not true. You just don't know it."

"What?" She was even more confused now, yet Arnold smirked beside her. He removed the crown and put it on Rishe's head instead.

"It looks better on you."

"Hey!"

"I'll take the blessing, though."

At least it wasn't a complete bother to him. Rishe smiled, relieved. "It looked quite lovely on you as well, Your Highness. You look so cute with flowers in your hair."

"Spare me."

"Oho, there's a face I don't see too often. I mean it! You *were* cute."

He snorted. "You are a fearless one, aren't you? I suppose you couldn't have bitten my neck if you weren't."

"Argh, you're bringing that up now?!" It was already becoming an embarrassing memory for Rishe. She hurriedly made excuses for herself. "You did it to me first!"

"I was saving your life. You had plenty of other options available to you."

"Ugh!" was the best retort she could muster. Arnold laughed again, amused. "You're proving my point about my string of losses."

"I told you, you're wrong about that."

Arnold ruffled Rishe's hair, apparently not intending to elaborate any more than that. She wanted to press the point, but she was far too distracted by the up-close view of his eyes.

I feel strange...

The pain in her chest was only getting worse. She couldn't help remembering their kiss in the chapel, and what Arnold had said to her then.

"You don't need to be resolute to become my wife."

Rishe clutched at her skirt and exhaled. There was a dull ache in her chest every time Arnold touched her. Why was that?

He once ran through this heart, and now it hurts.

It might even hurt more now than when he'd stabbed her. Arnold had whispered something to her in the last moments of her life as a knight. The memory was shrouded in dense fog, and she desperately wished to recall exactly what he'd said.

Rishe closed her eyes and pressed her forehead against Arnold's arm. She didn't want him to see her face, but she had to be natural about hiding it.

"What is it?"

"Just let me do this for a bit," she pleaded, almost a prayer. "I'm sleepy, so please lend me your shoulder, Your Highness."

Had Arnold realized she was lying? Even if he had, he said, "All right."

She sighed, leaning against him. He ran his fingers through her hair as if comforting a child.

Prince Arnold really is kind.

However, it didn't serve to alleviate her pain. It would have been nice if she'd actually gotten some sleep, but it wasn't to be. In the end, all Rishe could do was let the faintly sweet ache in her chest continue to torment her.

To be continued...

BONUS STORY

Without the Need for a Lullaby

THE NIGHT AFTER her encounter with the poisoned arrow in the forest, Rishe learned about Arnold's past and wept. Although she tried to keep the tears inside, they fell from her eyes anyway, unable to be contained. She burdened Arnold with her emotions and he wiped her eyes again and again, and after they'd done this for some time...

"Have you calmed down?"

"Yes." She nodded, sniffling, as Arnold stroked her hair. As she lay in bed, she gazed at the man beside her. Her head felt fuzzy, perhaps because of all the crying.

"Is there anything you want?"

Rishe pondered the question. She wasn't hungry. Her throat wasn't dry after drinking the antidote either. She knew the medicine was more effective the less fluids she had in her system, so she'd decided not to drink anything else.

While she thought about it, Arnold's fingers brushed against her neck. Well, more like the base of her skull, given that everything below was covered in bandages.

"Mm."

Arnold frowned. "Does it hurt?"

Rishe slowly shook her head and laid a hand on top of his, pressing his fingers to her neck. "Your hand is cold. It feels nice..."

His frown deepened. The fever ensured his cold skin really did feel good against hers. His big hand cupped her cheek; she felt like it stole away the fever's heat. Wanting more relief, she pressed into his hand. Arnold had a complicated look on his face, but he still let her do as she pleased. She couldn't keep him there forever, though.

"Thank you, Prince Arnold." Rishe nuzzled her cheek against his hand one last time, indulging in the comfortable coolness of his skin, then sighed. No matter how much she wished he would stay, she had to endure. She looked up at Arnold, eyelashes wet, and said, "I'm all right now. Please go back to your own room and get some rest."

Midnight was almost upon them, judging by the position of the moon in the sky. But Arnold's response was firm. "I can't just leave you alone."

He moved his hand down to hers on the bed and entwined their fingers. "I'll stay with you through the night," he said, voice heartbreakingly gentle.

"Ngh..." She knew it, she was making him worry. She couldn't let Arnold stay by her side; she worried over any lingering effects on him after he sucked the poison out, and she knew he was busy with work all of yesterday. If Arnold watched over Rishe, he would be the one falling ill next.

She attempted to sit up. "Y-you can't..."

"Rest."

"You need to rest too, Prince Arnold. I can't burden you any more than I already have."

"I'm not leaving. Go to sleep."

"Eep!" A gentle push against her shoulder was all it took to make her sink back into the bed.

His eloquent face said, *You don't even have the energy to sit up. What do you think you're doing?*

At this rate, he really will stay up all night. A creeping pain tightened around Rishe's heart at the thought. No supplement restored the body as well as sleep did. Staying up all night was damaging to the human constitution.

"Please, Prince Arnold!"

"I won't be granting any requests that will have a negative effect on your health."

"Ugh..." Her vision blurred again.

Arnold immediately grimaced. "I'm not budging on this even if it makes you cry."

"Th-then..." Rishe reached out and grasped Arnold's sleeve. "You get in bed too, Your Highness."

"What?"

"If you insist on staying in this room..." Her brain sluggish from all her crying, she desperately made her case to Arnold. "Then don't stay up all night. At least sleep here..."

The prince was momentarily speechless.

***

Arnold eventually relented to Rishe's half-crying tantrum. While his back was turned, Rishe slowly undressed, wiped her body down, and changed into a thin nightgown. Arnold wiped himself down as well, unbuttoning his shirt some, and then he was ready for bed.

Lying on the wall side of the bed, Rishe peered groggily at Arnold's back as he sat on the bed's edge. Even when he was just in his shirt, his back was so broad. His jacket made him look slender, but when he took it off, it was clear that he possessed a masculine build.

"Won't it be difficult to sleep if you don't return to your room and change into your bedclothes?"

Unbuttoning a cuff with one hand, he said, "I get the feeling you wouldn't let me back in if I left the room."

"..."

"I'll sleep like this."

He peeled back the bedspread. The springs creaked as the mattress sank beneath his weight. Rishe scooted closer to the wall, but Arnold said, "You don't need to move so far away."

Rishe, who lay on her side, examined Arnold's face after he rested his head on the pillow. It felt strange, sleeping in the same bed as someone else.

My head feels all fuzzy...

The bed was large; she would have to stretch her arm all the way out to reach him. Still worried, she asked, "It's not too cramped, is it?"

"It's fine."

"Really?" She pinched one of Arnold's sleeves and tugged it toward her, asking, "You're not pushing yourself because of my selfishness, are you?"

"I'm not, so don't cry."

Her thoughts were still in disarray, her mental state still fragile. Every little thing threatened to make her cry. She was sure she was being a terrible bother to Arnold.

Arnold was lying on his back, but he turned to face her instead, bringing them closer. He ran his fingers through Rishe's hair as if to comfort her. Even with her blurry vision, she could make out his troubled expression. His brow was the tiniest bit furrowed, but Rishe felt so bad, she blubbered.

"I'm sorry, Your Highness..."

"For what?"

"Well, it's like you have to care for a small child."

It certainly wasn't a task befitting a nation's crown prince, yet Arnold wasn't even angry with her about it.

"I don't think of you as a child."

What *did* he think of her as, then? She strained her exhausted mind and, regarding the hand in her hair, asked, "A pet, maybe?"

"Where did that come from?"

"Because, um..." She blinked slowly as she tried to vocalize her thoughts. "You're stroking my hair like you're petting me. It makes my heart all warm and fuzzy..." Rishe rubbed at her eye absentmindedly. Her thoughts were turning to mush.

"You must really be exhausted," Arnold said with some exasperation as he watched her.

"I'm not sleepy at all..."

"Right. Just close your eyes."

Rishe shook her head no. She was a little afraid to fall asleep. Arnold's hand pulled away as he sighed. Just as Rishe mourned the loss of his touch, he began to pat her lower back.

"Your Highness?" she blurted, blinking.

"Children fall asleep if you do this, right?"

Rishe gasped. Arnold had learned that from her. She slept in the same bed as Arnold, just like this, the day after Theodore caused the kidnapping fiasco. Back then, their positions had been reversed: Rishe had been the one lulling Arnold to sleep.

"But you just said I wasn't a child..."

"Did I?"

She tried to talk back to him, but the steady rhythm of his hand had clouded her thoughts even more.

"I-I'm not tired..." If she fell asleep now, she was worried Arnold would just get up again and watch over her. But she wouldn't mind if he fell asleep first, so she focused on him. "If I pat you, will you go to sleep first?"

"Why are you trying to make it a competition?"

"Mngh..."

Arnold was amazing. Her wavering emotions gradually steadied into a sleepy calm.

I can't fall asleep...not when I don't know if Prince Arnold will be able to get any rest...

She clutched Arnold's shirt so that he wouldn't be able to get out of the bed. Arnold frowned.

"Is that a habit of yours?"

"Hm?"

"You always try to pull whoever's next to you closer when you sleep."

In all honesty, she had no idea how to answer. This was her first time hearing it, and she hadn't a clue how such a habit had manifested when she'd never even slept with her own parents before.

"Last time, when I woke up, you were sleeping with your arms around my head."

Rishe blinked slowly. By "last time," he must have meant the other day when she'd soothed him to sleep. She remembered accidentally nodding off herself after Arnold had fallen asleep, but by the time she awoke, he'd already gotten out of bed.

"I don't remember that."

"I didn't think you would."

At any other time, she probably would have been shocked speechless—but her mind was still dull. She searched her vague memories and concluded she really didn't know what he was talking about.

"I think..." She tightened her grip on Arnold's shirt. "I probably wanted to protect you, Your Highness."

Arnold's hand stilled. He regarded Rishe like she was truly incomprehensible to him. "You don't need to protect me."

"But everyone's defenseless when they're sleeping."

When people slept, they were vulnerable. That was why Rishe couldn't sleep next to anyone. Fretting about something made it that much harder to doze off.

"Maybe I thought I could protect you if I was hugging you."

Arnold continued to stare.

As she nodded off, Rishe said, "If I can do it again today, maybe I'll fall asleep right away."

"You'll fall asleep in a minute no matter what I do."

Rishe felt frustrated, but sleep was winning out. She was still feverish, and she couldn't fight the lethargy much longer.

"Then..." Rishe let go of Arnold's shirt and pleaded in a quiet voice, "Can we hold hands instead?"

She'd never guessed how comforting it was to feel the warmth of another nearby. Though she didn't know if it was the exhaustion from so much crying or a spirit weakened by almost dying, she didn't feel like she could suppress her selfish desires at all. She craved his warmth and wanted him to stay, even if it was just until she fell asleep. That wish lingered in her heart as she gazed at him.

At last, Arnold wordlessly lowered his gaze and linked his fingers through hers. The way he held her hand was so tender and strong all at once. Rishe softly squeezed it.

Resigned and gentle, Arnold asked her, "Are you satisfied?"

"Hee hee hee..." Rishe beamed, delighted by the sense of security provided by their interlaced fingers. Before she could thank him, she ended up voicing her joy instead. "I'm very happy... I love it when you do this, Your Highness."

Arnold's hand was cold, but it quickly warmed in Rishe's. Enjoying the sensation, Rishe finally grew so tired, she couldn't stand it. Still, there was one thing she had to say.

"Promise me...you won't stay awake...after I fall asleep..."

Arnold sighed again. He shifted and brought his lips up to Rishe's ear, promising, "I'll sleep too."

"Right away?"

"Yeah. So don't worry."

She stopped resisting sleep then. Arnold wouldn't break a promise to Rishe. His actions had proven that.

"Good..." Her face relaxed into a dopey smile. She wanted to tell him "good night," but a powerful sleepiness stole away her consciousness. She let it go without a fight and fell dead asleep, still holding Arnold's hand.

Arnold heaved his biggest sigh of the day then, but of course Rishe didn't notice. She proceeded to enjoy pleasant dreams until the morning.

7th TIME LOOP
The Villainess Enjoys a Carefree Life
Married to Her Worst Enemy!

Afterword

TOUKO AMEKAWA here. Thank you so much for reading *7th Time Loop*, Volume 3!

This volume mostly centers around Rishe and the people she knew in her fourth life. I think Arnold and Rishe got a lot closer this time too. Arnold's open affection for Rishe is at about a four out of ten in this volume, so there's still plenty of room for him to grow! He's still got a lot of secrets, but I'll be happy if you'll continue to watch over him after this as well.

Thank you so much for the beautiful illustrations once again, Wan☆Hachipisu-sensei! I look at them over and over again every day. I'm obsessed. My eyes are in total bliss! To my proofreader, thank you for cleaning up all my various messes, and to my editor, thank you for putting up with all my unreasonable asks. I do feel remorse. I promise.

And most of all, I must thank my readers. Thank you for reading!

The manga version by Hinoki Kino-sensei is finally out now too. I'd love it if you checked out the lively adventures of Rishe and friends in the manga version! As for the novels, it seems I'll be able to get a fourth volume published. Nothing would make me happier than to be able to continue this relationship we have. I'll be praying we meet again in the next volume! Thank you once more.